I0667247

A ZEST FOR HAPPINESS

MELINA NARDI

Copyright © 2013 Melina Nardi

All rights reserved.

ISBN: 9563534425
ISBN-13: 978-956-353-442-9

In the rainy weather
In this world of loneliness
I got out of my house
And brought a bottle with me

I am still alive
So let me live
Let me drink in the rain

I don't want to live in pieces
I don't want to drink drop by drop

Take away the glasses
Bring me the whole tavern

- **Baarsat Ke Mausam Mein -**

"Naajayaz"

ACKNOWLEDGMENTS

To all those who get out of their houses and refuse to live their lives in pieces.

To my parents, who gave me my passion for traveling and never failed to believe in me.

To the people who shared with me their stories and inspired me to write about those lives so often ignored and forgotten.

1989

1- NEITHER THE WINDS NOR THE BLOWS

Chargulli, Northern Pakistan, 1989

- " Chipcha! Kunna sor!" Shush, sit down!

- "But… baba?!"

The man had big hands showing signs of hardship. Sameer covered his face with his own tiny hands, where each scar was the mark of a small mischief. The most recent scar was still slightly bleeding in the spot where the chicken had planted its beak. It was him who had convinced the "gang" to go for the bird. Under his orders, Najib had positioned himself right around the house corner, checking for signs of life and unwanted arrivals. Qasim was in charge of grabbing the bird, and Sameer was put ready to receive the package, hide it in his *chader* and run away as fast as he could, the chicken yapping and flapping strong in its folds. As usual, the plan worked to perfection, and the kicking and beaking of the chicken was not enough to discourage Sameer who could only think of the sumptuous meal Qasim's sister would be preparing that same evening. She'd kill the beast herself, tear off the feathers, and separate the meat into pieces, leaving the insides – the liver, the heart and the stomach – for later consumption. She would put these to macerate for days, letting them impregnate with spices and oil. Only the thighs and breast would be boiled in curry water and devoured right away. Chicken and tomatoes. A feast of tender meat the three boys had been dreaming of for the past two weeks.

Once a month, each of the town's family would select its biggest chicken and tie it up for days to reduce the muscles and increase the fatty parts. Yet, even a chicken the size of a watermelon would not get very far in a family of ten. Once prepared with plenty of vegetables, beans and spices by Sameer's sisters, each member of the family would be given an equal amount of meat: a few pieces lost in the broth of tomatoes, peppers, potatoes and ginger.

Today though, the gang had feasted on a whole chicken, just for themselves, and now Sameer was facing the consequences. It was his fault: he had not been prudent enough and was starting to make a bad reputation for himself. He had nearly been caught stealing potatoes a few times, and once an old *naani* had managed to recognize him before he could grab her biggest chicken. Instead of crouching down just below the house's windows, slowly advancing towards the barn like a cautious feline, Sameer had panicked, running as fast as he could, determined to grab and go before the old lady could even stand up from the bag of potatoes where she'd generally sit all day, peeling onions and cooking washed-up dishes for a defunct husband. She had spotted him from a window and – surprisingly agile - burst out of her house shouting to the chicken "Hush! Go home! Go home!". Waking up from his nap, the bird raised an alarmed head then ran to his wooden henhouse in a shambles of feathers and screams. Qasim and Najib, guarding the entrance, stood there laughing at the sight of the old lady shrieking and spitting, Sameer running and swearing, and the chicken flapping around "Ekh Ekh Ekh!"

Qasim and Najib left with their reputation untouched, but Sameer had now become the Number One suspect in all cases of chicken disappearance. So when the voice of a new chicken theft spread from old shrew mouths' to young gossipy girl ears', it made no doubt to anybody that Sameer was behind the crime.

* * *

Hamid Ahmadi – who was now buoying up a threatening hand over his child's head – had always refused to hurt his progeny in any way, but tonight he was nervous and on edge. Like every day, he had gone to the communal room where the whole quarter meets daily to gossip, play cards, talk politics, and smoke hashish. When he arrived the crowd was debating vividly. The Afghan Army had just recaptured Samarkhel from the hands of the mujahideen.

Samarkhel stood just a few kilometers southeast of Jalalabad, and was particularly dear to the old Major. A few years before Sameer was born, Hamid had left the Laghman Province, just north of Jalalabad, to cross the Pakistani border in search of safety and quiet. This was in the early 1980s, when the Soviets had just started invading Afghanistan. Hamid – who was a man of little education but grounded common sense – felt that an army of infidels preaching equality and absolute public property could not be the bearer of any good news. Not that he was very religious himself, but he knew his compatriots well, and he knew that they would not surrender to a power that invalidated their entire system of beliefs without fighting hard. Bigotry and social inequality were so well rooted in his companions' culture, that, according to Hamid, "they could not recognize freedom even if it came punching them in the face". So Hamid and his wife left for Chargulli, where an uncle would take them under his roof.

There were no more than 280 kilometers between Mehter Lam in the northeast of Afghanistan, and Chargulli in the north of Pakistan. Still, that trip was the most dangerous project Hamid had undertaken in his entire life. One had to be pretty desperate – or pretty visionary – to dare take that path. At the time, most Afghanis thought that the Russians would give up within a year, having lost interest in colonization after admiring the Pathan strength and devotion. Only a handful of businessmen and illuminated philosophes dared suggesting a lengthy invasion. Hamid was neither, but "never fight from the pit, son! Always look to attack from above" – had repeated his father all his life. Even on his death-bed, while the women were already chanting the ritualistic hymn, he had whispered in Hamid´s ear: "never from the pit, son! Never from the pit."

After waiting in vain for two weeks in Jalalabad to be taken to Pakistan by some intrepid truck driver ready to risk his life for a few rupees, the Ahmadi family decided to try their luck in Samarkhel where, supposedly, more smugglers could be found. In the crowded streets of Samarkhel a wind – or really just a breeze – of freedom was already blowing, ruffling the hijabs of the legions of young women who were now taking to the schools, hailing communism for opening them the doors of education. A fragile murmur of freedom which had brought to him the mother he had never had: Chereen, their hostess.

She came from Kabul; she must have been forty, maybe more, maybe less. Her husband had died only a year after marrying her, leaving her widowed at eighteen, and childless. From then on, she'd earned a living hosting limbo passengers, lost in between two front lines, waiting for destiny to show them the way. She'd give them a roof, motherly protection, and, sometimes, if the month had been rough and the traveler insisted just hard enough, she'd give that much more of herself in exchange for a few extra rupees. She'd never thought she'd come down to that, yet times were hard and she was an unaccompanied woman sharing her living space with unrelated men. She could read in her neighbors' eyes despise, reprobation, disgust even. She had been considered the town's shameful promiscuous whore the minute she had let the first traveler in. So who cared at that point?

By the light of the moon fading behind the mountains, Chereen would tell Hamid and his wife about the marvels and follies of the big city. She had left Kabul in 1978, right after the President Sardar Muhammad Daud Khan had been deposed by Noor Mohammed Taraki, who started the Marxist reforms. "Good for him!" she would shout, referring to Taraki's assassination a few months earlier, in September 1979. Chereen hated anything and everything that would remind her of the Soviets. Her dad had been draught to fight against the Chechen and had never come back. Whether he had been taken by a bullet or a Russian prostitute, she never knew. "But that's another story" she would declare every time she even came near the subject. She would then go on describing Kabul and praising President Daud whom, she'd say, saved the country from being plunged and dried up by the monarchy. Right: not only did Chereen hate communism, she also hated kings and princes as much as liberals and hippies. "Kabul", she'd ramble, "used to be full of potheads". Ten years later, the hippies had gone, leaving room to liberated women wearing skirts and painting their nails. The communists were even having them work in public administrations! If she despised communism, Chereen couldn't help but envy those women and wish, deep down, that she could join their ranks. Sure, Samarkhel was already too far from the capital to suffer (enjoy?) its influence, but somehow – she'd say with a certain mischievous light – even imperceptibly, one could feel a mild breeze swooshing under the girls' dresses and into the young people's minds.

Hamid had spent three weeks in Samarkhel – preparing every detail of the trip, learning every curve of the path, and observing the few tiny changes already swirling their way over from Kabul.

In Mehter Lam, kilometers away from civilization, stories were being told of entire families who had disappeared crossing the border hidden in empty gasoline tanks. The fumes of the gasoline stuck on the walls of the tank would slowly suffocate them, and if the truck didn't make it in time, they'd be found dead, huddled together, black from the sticky liquid. Not often would the truck driver bother returning the corpses to their family – rarely would he even know his passengers' real names.

Since they did not have children with them, Hamid could more easily hide under a Burqa, tagging along a caravan, pretending to be some trader's wife. Not that the solution was much less dangerous – but Hamid preferred to die smashed into the ground than suffocated by poisonous fumes.

Then the day came, when the caravan was ready and the die was cast. Hamid was about to face God in a game of chess where God was the King and he was a mere peon.

The path taken by those caravans of peasants and donkeys ran high in the mountains of the Kuz Kunar district. They followed the Kunar-Bajaur link road for about fifty kilometers, but not lounging the Kunar River as they'd be exposed to the attacks of the tribes living in the mountains of the Ghaziabad district. Rather they climbed up the mountains of the Nangarhar district, hiding as they may. They crossed the border using a path forged through the years only by the feet of the peasants endangering their life many times a year to go and sell their goods in Peshawar, and by the clogs of the donkeys, sternly dragging the rugs delicately made by famished little hands. It took nearly a week for Hamid and his wife to cross the seventy kilometers separating them from the border, and another week still to reach Ghalanai in the Tribal Areas of Pakistan.

After Ghalanai, they travelled to Shabqadar where their main concern was to evade the Pakistani patrols. Passed Shabqadar, Hamid and his wife let the traders take south to Peshawar, while they followed east to Mardan, still hiding under their Burqa. From Shabqadar they walked another 89 kilometers before finally reaching

Chargulli where – as Hamid had hoped – uncle Mahmoud welcomed them and offer them a safer life. Hamid was determined to find a good job and work hard so that they could soon settle in their own home. Then, Hamid would give his wife many beautiful children; little replicas of himself to lighten up their life and build the Ahmadi name after his death.

Nine years after, finally, Hamid was listening to the news of the Soviets' withdrawal. February 15, 1989, the last of the Soviet troops had retrenched to a defeated Soviet Union, leaving the Afghan Government alone against the mujahedeen. President Mohammad Najibullah had already declared the state of emergency, removing any non-communist minister. The Marxist Democratic Republic of Afghanistan was to remain heavily funded by the Soviet Union, which also provided food and military supplies for Najibullah to continue the fight against the American-backed mujahedeen.

Half of Chargulli was glued to its radio transistors, listening patiently as Samarkhel was being rocked back and forth between both fronts, ploughed by both sides, the women oscillating between days of freedom and nights of repression. They were Pathan families from the provinces of Langham, Kunar, Kapisa in northern Afghanistan... all of them longing to return to their familiar mountains and greener pastures.

Faithful and optimistic, Hamid's companions were already restlessly ordering their wives around, exhausted little hamsters packing and sweating, cooking and sweating, all day long sweating while their husbands planned on their looming return to homeland. They wanted to believe that the fight would be brief, that the US troops would be kind, that the winds would be favorable. They all sighed at a time when Kabul was full of potheads, not soldiers, and their lands full of vegetables, not landmines. Hamid, alone, was neither faithful nor optimistic. He sure wasn't feeling relieved! Quite to the contrary, he had this annoying conviction that now that the Afghans had lost their common enemy, it was only a matter of time before they started turning against each other.

The thought was still hovering in his mind when his hand fell down on Sameer's right cheek, then returned back to hit the other side like a whip.

* * *

Sameer woke up the next morning with the cheeks still burning from the slap, but he didn't care. Today the gang had a new mission: apple picking. It was the beginning of the summer and the trees were now heavy with fruits so sweet and juicy that it felt like liquor in their veins. This time Sameer was commanding the operations. He had managed to hide in his pockets pieces of dried meat and had spent some time spying on the ferocious dog, which was put to guard the apple trees. The dog often fell asleep around 2pm, when the sun was high and the midday prayer was over. The attack was set.

The three boys arrived as the dog was laying head between paws, half alert, half in a gaze. Sameer jumped the small stonewall first and ran to the tree, climbed with the ability of a monkey and reached for the shiniest apples. Qasim and Najib stood below, intercepting the apples and filling their *chader* as fast they could before the growls of their impatient stomachs would awake the beast. Perched in the tree, Sameer saw it first. The dog opened an eye, than the other, and detecting an abnormal presence rose to its full height, lifted the chin and exposed a terrifying range of pointy teeth in a growl of anger. Without even daring a look, Qasim and Najib took to run, each in opposite directions, the apples jumping around in their *chaders*, their hearts beating strong in their chests, and the dog running around behind them. Sameer threw the provisions of dried meat all at once at the dog, already fleeing the scene and thanking God for the hours of soccer practice in the mud fields. Sameer was running fast and steady straight to his house, where he precipitated onto his mattress, hiding like a criminal under the heavy cotton covers.

From under the blanket, Sameer could hear the voices of his familiars discussing the latest events. He was only nine but already he could sense the concern in his father's tone. As an officer in the Pakistani Air Force, Hamid Ahmadi was well informed on the State's affairs. He nurtured a particular interest for the Pakistan Atomic Energy Commission and for its chairman, Munir Ahmed Khan, whom he considered the "father of Pakistan's atomic bomb project". Just as most Afghan refugees in Chargulli, Hamid was convinced that atomic power would ensure that the Soviets, the Yankees and all those greedy world powers would finally stay away from their land, allowing them to fantasize about an imminent return to their homeland.

- "That's it, we don't have to fear anyone now! Munir Ahmed Khan has been dealing with the West Germans to import tritium recovery equipment. The PAEC did some tests in Pinstech's center, near Rawalpindi, no later than yesterday… everything is ready, they say."
- "I heard that the US secretly complained to West Germany, asking them to cease the exportation of heavy water purification materials to Pakistan."
- "Kha kha, but they can't prove any nuclear use of the purification plant, so they cannot do anything against the PAEC".

- "Did you know that the Germans are also exporting beryllium to India? With that they can construct bombs faster than us!"
- "That's fine, they can try, but we have China on our side! Last month a bunch of Chinese scientists visited the Khan Research Laboratories in Kahuta and now some of our scientists are going to visit their test center in Lop Nur."
- "Plus we have the Islamic bomb! Our is Hallal! Ah-ah-ah!"

In between the laughs and the jokes, Sameer discerned the unraveling of a story much bigger than what any of them could comprehend. He had heard his father talking about the Pinstech center and the PAEC many times… Lately, these names had come up every time his dad would invite friends over. Shazmina would disappear in the kitchen, striving to escape her husband's lengthy conversations, trying to ignore all the dangers surrounding her family, but the curtains were too thin and the men would ramble on and on… something about a bomb able to erase the whole of Chargulli from the face of the earth. Sameer didn't like those discussions. It always ended with some grand speech on how – one day – Afghanistan would be great again, and how Pakistan would help the Mujahedeen sweep communism out of Afghanistan and restore Islam in the nation. Although his dad would always talk about Afghanistan as his "home", Sameer had a hard time considering himself an Afghan. Pakistani, Afghan, Pathan… it all became confused in his head.

- "Isn't Chargulli our home, baba?" Sameer had asked the first time he had heard his father talk about *back home*.

- "Our blood is our home, son. Wherever we are together, we are home. Our ancestors resided in Afghanistan. There they lived and there they rest. Until we are separated from them, we are like plants without their roots. Without roots, how will we grow? Soon we will go back to live all together in Afghanistan, you'll see, because that is where we belong."

- "But we're together here. Can't we stay here? I like it here."

- "I know, son. You're too young to understand. One day, you'll understand what it means to be a Pathan. Everybody respects us for our strength. Whatever happens, we never cry, we never beg. Neither the winds nor the hits: we never break. Don't you ever forget that, son: you're a Pathan. Nobody can break a Pathan!"

But Sameer felt nothing like a Pathan. He felt tears tickling his eyes, and a strong desire to beg his father to quit the Air Force and never leave them ever again. He was terrified at the idea that his father could be called to fight for Pakistan against the government of Najibullah. He understood nothing of politics but he knew of war. His grandfather had fought in the British Army against the Germans in Japan and Sameer's childhood had been filled with the stories of his combats. Under the petrol lamp in the unique bedroom where all would gather to prepare for the night, Sameer's *dada* would relate episodes of his life as a soldier. Tucked under the blanket, so heavy that he could barely move, Sameer would listen, fascinated, stories of heroes, blood and victories. He loved those stories, but to think of his father in such a war… this he would rather not think about at all. Besides, there was a much more urgent matter for the time being… He hadn't tasted apples since the previous autumn and now it felt like ages since the last bite. In his throat he could already feel dropping the sweet and sour liquid. Sameer left the bombs and wars behind and rushed to meet Qasim and Najib at the Kalu Khan Bridge, the gang's usual hiding spot. With the stomach in agony, he reached to Ali Baba's cavern where the pair of vultures was already happily devouring the profits of their larceny.

* * *

As the summer was slowly coming to an end, the suspicions were rising on the gang. They had managed to steal from everything: apples, chickens, watermelons, cucumbers. Yet, they had also become infamous since Sameer was discovered, and the other two were soon suspected by association. It was becoming harder and harder for the boys to find sources of nutritional pleasures without risking their reputations. Qasim, who was the cunning one, came up with an idea. "Let's go and get some scrap metal to sell! In the field next to my family's, there's an old unused telephone pole. The field has recently been plowed so it's softer and easier to move. Let's take the pole out, cut it, and sell the pieces!"

Around 11pm the next night, the three scoundrels sneaked out in the dark and tiptoed to the pole armed only of their bare hands and youthful determination. They dug the soil for a bit then started rocking the pole back and forth to slowly free it from the ground. What they had not predicted, though, was that the pole not only was filled with cement at its bottom, but was also surrounded by a cement cap that made it much harder to plug out. After fifteen minutes of meticulous rocking, the freshly plowed soil finally gave up, letting the pole out of his cage and down to lay on the ground.

- "This damn thing is too heavy! You two get the bottom part, and I'll carry the front on my own" said Qasim - who was also the strong one.

- "Huuuh – humph", and up with the pole.
- "Argh – Aaaouuuuuch", and down went the pole, right on Sameer's right ankle.

His foot stuck under the cement layer, Sameer was cursing and whining, suddenly realizing that the tricks and the grown-up games had not yet taken the boy out of him. Yes he felt like crying for his mama, but the pathan pride prevented him. So he bit his lips and promptly reached a safe spot as the other two dragged the pole away. The rest of the journey home was completed by Qasim and Najib, lifting the pole up, moving it a few feet further, and throwing it back on the ground, won over by the weight.

- "It'd better be worth at least 400 rupees!" kept growling Najib who could feel his muscles burning like the strings of a *rubab* after a wedding.

Sameer was limping on the side, trying to appear stoic and not to show his disappointment. He was already considered as the baby of the group because he was a few months younger than the other two, so he had been striving to show his worth. Now everything was ruined. Unless... unless he managed to regain his position by organizing a raid onto the nearby sugarcane depot. Their families rarely had money for sugar or honey, so the only sweetness they tasted came from fruits. Sugarcane would be like *Eid* in July! By the time they got to Qasim's field and hid the pole under leaves and earth for the night, Sameer had the whole plan set up and was already all pumped up.

The next morning, Sameer woke up with an ankle big as a melon. There was no time to be a sissy though. The boys were counting on him to help them cut the pole before they got spotted. Considering the size of the tube, it would take a while and three pairs of hands would be needed. On one foot, Sameer hopped to the back of the house where his father kept the axes.

- "Cherta ze?"

Shazmina was looking at her son with knowing eyes. Sameer was convinced that mums always know everything – no matter how much he would hide, she would always know what sort of shenanigans he was concocting. Her half-angry – half-amused look confirmed his doubts.

- "Sta se kai ma bachey?" What are you up to, my son?

And she pointed straight at his ankle with the menacing look of a war dog.

- "I slipped in a hole, mama!"

Shazmina called the family healer, the *naanii*, who sat him down on the floor and examined the red and yellow fruit blossoming on his ankle. She spat a few times on it, then applied some ointment and tied around it a special *taweez* she had made herself. On a piece of paper she had written incantations against demons and evils spirits only she knew about. She had then minutely folded the paper into a small square, trapping it between two squares of black leather which she stitched together. She also recommended days of rest at home and lots of green tea, but Sameer was in no mood to listen. He was in a hurry and knew his friends would scold him if he didn't show up.

After his *naani* finished the ritual, she called all the women into the kitchen and resolved to prepare her secret healing soup. Since times could recall, women in her family had transmitted that recipe to their female progeny through a coded song that was kept unintelligible to men. The authenticity of the recipe was doubtful but the only belief of its power was often sufficient enough to cure the worst of evils. Sameer took advantage of their diverted attention to disappear. Hopping and skipping he rushed to the field, holding the ax hidden under his qamees.

In three, the boys managed to chop the pole down in no time, they piled it in their *chader,* which they tied onto the back of a donkey they had rented from a clueless old man. Qasim was to take it to a special contact of his in the city: a guy who he knew would give good cash and ask no questions. His father was a merchant and Qasim often helped him in the shop, selling soap, batteries, socks, a few groceries… well, pretty much anything they could find in Peshawar and pack up on the roof of their rusted Suzuki FX. Thanks to the shop, Qasim knew everybody in the whole of Chargulli and always had the best contacts even for the shadiest of businesses. Affairs done, Sameer went back home, plunged into bed and fell asleep like a stone, won over by the pain and his grandma's magic.

Outside a shove of wind took the first leaf off the biggest tree, whisking it softly to the ground, silently announcing the end of the summer. Far in the distance, a few gunshots echoed, followed by manly grunts and a chorus of fearless cries: "Allahu Akbar. Allahu Akbar!"

Homeland was calling.

2- SMELLS OF RAGÚ AND TASTE OF BLOOD

Naples, Italy, 1989

Nicola had big blue eyes. Maybe they weren't so big. Maybe it was just an impression. He always was a curious soul. He'd look at the sky and wonder about how long his arm should be so he could touch it. He'd look at ants running from the rain and imagine what would be the impact of a drop of heavy rain falling on the back of a tiny black ant. He didn´t think about it in mathematical term, no. At nine, Nicola still had a hard time accepting things could be divided and subtracted so easily.

-   "If Marcello has five thousand Lira, and Mario takes a thousand Lira from him, what is Marcello left with?"

Sorrow? Pain? A beating from his mother? No dinner? The teacher would end up crying in despair.

- "Four thousand Lira, Nicola! He's left with four thousand Lira!"

How can you take away a thousand lira from a child's pocket, probably condemning him to a good beating – if this boy's mum was anything like his, she'd probably send him to his room with a kick in the ass! How can you steal from this boy and pretend that the important thing is that he still has four thousand Lira left?

- "If my friend took away my money", would he retort to Miss Marialisa, "I'd feel sad. And then I'd feel angry and I'd beat him up to teach him!"

Miss Marialisa would sigh and send him home. Nicola drove her crazy – especially every time she tried teaching him maths – but he was a good boy and she had a particular sweet spot for him. Sometimes, she felt like he was right after all. Mathematics simplified life way too much. Never a subtraction was as easy and innocent as 2 minus 1. With a subtraction, somebody always ended up being hurt, something would go missing. What happened to that 1 that was taken away? Mathematics would never say. It disappeared. Nobody but Nicola seemed to care. That's why she cared for him so much, maybe more than the other boys. She always gave him bad grades reluctantly, but rules were rules, and Marialisa had been taught to respect the rules. She'd been taught to say "Buongiorno, Signore" and "Buona notte, Comandante". She'd been taught to talk like a true lady by a father who never recovered from losing the war.

The day they hanged Mussolini up by his feet in Piazzale Loreto, on April 29, 1945, Marialisa's father – Domenico - had travelled all the way to Milan to show him his respect. When he saw him dangling up there, his lover Claretta Petacci next to him, and the crowd hissing, spitting, and bowing, throwing rocks, and even their own shoes, at him, he cried wholeheartedly. He was a boy then. He thought of fascism as order, fairness, reliability; a light at a time he had felt lost and lonely.

* * *

Domenico Donato came from humble roots. On a cold and gloomy day of 1924, his mother had delivered him on the very straw she had collected that morning. She had breastfed him on the same chair, at the same corner of the fireplace, every morning for the next year. Domenico had grown to be a vivid young man in the outskirts of Naples, day after day taking care of the pigs and chickens, watering the lettuces and onions, trimming the vines and the roses. He worked every day like a mule – or at least that was how he felt, powerless in front of his parents' conviction that education was of no use.

- "That northern dialect they call *Italiano*, what a joke! Why would you study it, huh, if it will never take over our beautiful Neapulitan? Let them fool themselves with their dreams of grandeur. We got everything we need right here, don't we?"

Domenico's father would never change his mind. It was what it was.

At the age of sixteen, Domenico escaped from the farm. He ran for days, till he got to Naples and there found a carriage on its way to Rome. With the money stolen from his old man, he survived a few days, but was soon left with nothing, alone, speaking a language nobody even understood. He went from bar to bar looking for a job until, one day, a tall man with a black Borsalino turned to him and saw something in him, not even Domenico knew was there.

Leccisi was an educated man and he liked Domenico because he was so eager to learn. He took him in, gave him a job and a roof, and introduced his new protégé to the light of fascism. He taught him proper Italian and inculcated him with the true values that Italy stood for. How they came from the Romans and how Rome used to be a great empire, which had the whole world at its feet. The summer of 1940 was expanding its wings of heat, and Italy was about to be drawn into war, yet Leccisi made sure Domenico would only see it from afar, maintaining intact his pure virgin spirit.

Domenico was taught to be a proud fascist by a man who believed in order and rules before anything else. Order and rules made him feel safe, as if he could predict everything that would happen because it was all coded and mapped. It seemed logical too that everybody had to abide by the same rules. Domenico had seen a black man once. He was so dark – like he had just returned from the depth of Hell – that everybody stopped to look at him. Little boys would surround him for a chance to touch him and mothers would run alerted after them to protect their progeny from that creature of the Devil. Within a few seconds it was chaos in via Milano. That day, Domenico understood what his mentor would say about foreigners. It wasn't really a question of what they thought or did, it was a question of disrupting the perfect order of things, bringing confusion in the women's hearts and curiosity in the children's minds. Foreigners just didn't belong in the new Roman Empire. The same applied to communists and liberals, and conservatives – of course. They all had crazy ideas that were oh-so very dangerous for the stability of ITALIA. Domenico loved it when Leccisi would tell him about *Italia*. One nation under which all were united. All spoke the same language and shared the same culture and ideology. Soon, France, Austria and Germany would fall in love with the beauty of *Italia* and beg to join. And so the great Roman Empire would rise from its ashes.

When Mussolini talked to the labor forces in late 1943 to explain that they too were to be part of the unification process and that he was going to help them by nationalizing all enterprises of more than a hundred employees, Domenico stood and applauded. He thought about his parents on the outskirts of Naples and wondered what they had become. He felt happy at the thought that they too could be part of a strong and admirable fascist Italy.

Just a year later, though, everything started to fall apart. Domenico realized that Mussolini's populist speech was just a sham. He started hearing conversations about Mussolini being Hitler's puppet. He overheard talks about Mussolini's poor health. Some said Hitler forced him to set up the Italian Social Republic and was now using him as a personal shoe-shiner. Against his will, Mussolini had ceded Istria, Trieste and South Tyrol to the Führer. "There is nothing grand about Mussolini anymore", an old man said at a table next to them, just as Leccisi raised his glass to toast to his pupil's 20th birthday. The restaurant was fancy and the crowd polite. They all turned and hid their opened mouth behind their gloved hands as they witnessed Domenico jump out of his seat, stand in front of the grey-haired man and slap him across the face with all the strength of his youthful convictions.

Over the following months, everything went down fast. Hitler was losing on the Russian front and Mussolini was desperately battling against the Allies in the South. Some rumors were starting to be heard about what fascist factions were doing to war prisoners in Salò, on the borders of Lake Guardia, where Mussolini had established his headquarters. Everywhere Domenico would go, caffè, bar, barber, he would hear new horrible news about the Nazis. Italy was helping Hitler kill millions, Mussolini would barely ever appear in public anymore and Fascist factions were torturing for pleasure. Where was the order in all that?

On April 25, 1945, the Repubblica Sociale d'Italia came to an end, Leccisi disappeared, and Domenico had no idea what to think or do. He took a train to Milan to see the Duce dangling on the pole of an old gas station and there, in the middle of the crowd, he cried out of shame, frustration, confusion, and sorrow. He cried upon the Dictator's tragic end, and upon his own miserable faith.

In April 1946, Leccisi reappeared only to request his help in moving the Duce's body. Domenico Donato was right next to Leccisi when they exhumed the lifeless body of Benito Mussolini from its grave in Musocco. He was there to watch over the body while they kept it in secret in Madesimo, and he was there when the Cappucini monks took it to their monastery.

After a year of depression, the secret operation had brought him some light. He had to bring order back into his life in his own way. The next day he applied to the La Sapienza University of Rome, Department of Law. There he met crystalline Rosalina who loved things to be tidied up and always had a hairdo perfectly in place. Domenico lived happy for a few years. He would wake up at 7am sharp every morning and find his espresso ready on the kitchen table, together with his newspaper and his work papers perfectly ordered. Despite his young age he was very successful in his office. He was so scrupulous he never missed a fact or a piece of evidence. At 1:40pm on the dot he would get home to find a plate of smoking lasagna like only Rosalina could cook – with every layer of pasta exactly equidistant from the others. Then, one day, he got a call to his office from his mother-in-law. Rosalina was in labor. By the time he reached the hospital, Rosalina's body was lying lifeless, her white hand still holding the tiny body of delicate Marialisa. From that moment, Domenic's only source of happiness in life was the idea that he was able to pass onto his daughter his dreams of an Italy where trains arrived on time, buildings remained perfectly white, and people could understand each other from the Apennine Mountains all the way to the Ionian Sea.

* * *

Despite Domenico's best efforts, Marialisa grew up to be a vagabond and a dreamer. At the age of twenty, Marialisa fell in love with a handsome man from Bologna whom she followed all the way there. In Bologna, she took up studying literature and lived passionately with her Adonis for a couple of years. Bologna became for her the place of her spiritual birth. She could feel her spirit burgeoning day after day, pulsing stronger and stronger as a constant flow of beauty, music and philosophy impregnated her. She'd sit for hours on the stairs of the San Petronio church. She'd sense at her back the protection of the imposing construction. The lowest part, covered in white and pink marble was the feminine hug of the mother she had never known. The marble, warmed by the sun would whisper stories of mothers hugging their children or dragging them along to mass. As if cut in two, the highest part of the church was left naked, its wooden wall exhibiting itself, indecent, unfinished. In front of her, San Petronio himself would raise his hand to offer his benediction. Even years after, Marialisa never forgot the smells and the colors – how everything would turn red in the late afternoon: the sky, the walls, the people. Bologna la Rossa, Bologna la Ghiotta, Bologna la Dotta. Bologna the Red, the Glutton, the Erudite. She could close her eyes and let her mind walk through the narrow streets, recognizing every statue, every hidden alcove, every little boutique. She'd wander again by the Bottega Instabile, a corner shop devoted to the desires of its patrons. A place to sit and talk, paint or write, or to learn some new engraving technique. And she'd reminisce sometimes over how she'd stop by, just to taste a new wine with

Niccolò, the owner, and the night would expand into the wee hours of the morning, ending only when the last feeling was exposed, when the last project was conceived. She had planted a few basil and rosemary plants there, leaving pieces of herself in various parts of the city. A plant at the Bottega, a dance at the Arteria, or a prayer at Santa Lucia, perched on the hills of Bologna. Pieces that went on living even after she left, horrified and betrayed.

Lost in her avid contemplation of the city, Marialisa never saw it coming. She never noticed anything. She was in love; a bit naive too. On the first day of August, 1980, her handsome man from Bologna told her he had to leave: a very important mission to fulfill… *she wouldn't understand*. He hugged her for a very long time, grabbed a backpack and disappeared down the stairs of the building. On August the 2nd at 10:25am, the 2nd-class waiting room of Bologna's train station blew up, killing eighty-five persons and seriously injuring two hundred. The same day she took a bus back to Rome and left behind every memory of that treacherous love. She never knew why he and his accomplices did it; some said they were some sort of neo-fascists attacking the communist bastion that was Bologna. Others talked of a pro-Palestinian group, others sustained that they were nothing more than nut-jobs from some kind of extreme right movement. Marialisa didn't care. She was certain that the man she had loved was part of it and she hated him and herself for that. Seeing her pain, Domenico Donato convinced a friend to get his daughter a job as a primary school teacher in Napoli. Marialisa had never finished her studies and knew little of sciences, but she took to it without thinking twice. Nine years later, she was still teaching with the same joy and passion. She had seen her first students become young men thirsty for obtaining the laurel crown of knowledge from the best universities in the country. This year she was faced with a new challenge: a sweet little dreamer with big blue eyes. She couldn't wait to see what kind of an amazing person he would grow up to be.

* * *

- "Nico, che stai a guarda accusì figliu mie?"

On his way home from school, Nicola had remained entranced with the show inside the pizzeria "Da Beppe". Beppe was the pizzaiolo. Despite his disdain for hygiene, everybody in the decrepit Neapolitan neighborhood of the Quartieri Spagnoli considered him the best pizzaiolo in town. He made pizzas dance in the air with an elegance and delicacy that strangely contrasted with the roundness of his belly tight up in a greasy tank-top tucked in dirty blue jeans. Nicola was standing on the tip of his toes, trying to get his head over the counter to get a full view of the show. He was observing with attention every movement of the dough, trying to imagine how it felt to be ploughed and smashed, then caressed and kneaded, but then smashed again onto the white marble. In his mind, every emotion of the dough came in slow motion. Its surprise under the first grasp, its frustration maybe at the beginning and then its slow abandon to the loving hands of its master, till the moment of the elevation, when everything became part of the universe, the dough being part of the flow of life, the pizzaiolo the god which ordained elements and decided upon destinies. With his heavy hands covered in flour, he raised a ladle full of *passata* and drew circles of red in a perfect continuous gesture. Slices of mozzarella from Caserta, white and creamy, and a few cherry tomatoes cut in half… all offered as if an ancient ritual to the heat of the massive wood stove.

- "Nico!"

- …

- "Nicolaaaa!"

- "A mamme'te te sta a chiama', Nico! Mo' ve'te a ca', vaiul!

As far as Beppe was concerned, Angela was a piece of candy he'd love to chew on… but she was way out of his reach – first because she was beautiful and he was… well… out of shape; then because she was married to Don Mario: the charm of a Marcello Mastroiani with the influence and power of a Don Corleone. As for Nicola, though, his mum was a two-headed monster who hated being disobeyed. His many escapades and foolish tricks were inevitably gratified with a spanking before being sent to bed with no dinner. A monster indeed, but still he preferred the reprimands of his mother to the absence of his father. Sure his dad was a big shot in town and because of that everybody would always treat Nicola like a prince. Don Mario's boy they'd call him, and they'd stuff him with pie, frittata di maccheroni, and – his favorite – the Neapolitan babà! "Don Mario's boy, my ass!" thought Nicola. "The only time Don Mario remembers he has a boy is at events and parties, when he shows me around like I'm a dog, repeating to everybody *Sara' cum a me sta criature! A future Don, glielu dico io!*" What that meant, Nicola had no idea. Yet he got one thing straight for sure: he'd never be like his dad. "A future Don, my ass!" he'd murmur to himself.

- "We, Nicuuu! Ven a ca' e ca nun teng ca dirtelo chiu!"

Nicola jumped out of his musing, thanked Beppe who was taking out of the oven a perfect pizza Margarita (the cheese was bubbling and the crust looked perfectly crispy). Nicola took a second to admire yet another work of art from Beppe before running out of the door, into the front building, up the stairs all the way to the 4th floor where he found his mum in the kitchen, a wooden spoon in one hand and an angry look on her face. She banged a plate of smoking pasta onto the kitchen table and stood there watching him eat. On the TV, the only color TV in the neighborhood (those were the perks of having a mafia boss for a father), the news started but Nicola wasn't listening. Rather he was conscientiously eating his pasta, tasting the sweetness of the tomatoes, the freshness of the basil, the saltiness of the Parmigiano and the smooth yet not too smooth texture of the tagliatelle. It was perfect. There was nothing like his mum's pasta. Nothing. Suddenly he realized Angela was now sitting too, watching – livid – the TV screen. Curious and a bit worried, Nicola started watching too. They were talking of a wall, showing images of people sitting on top, laughing, and others taking bits of it out and making holes. The camera showed the hole and you could see there were people on the other side, laughing and shouting. Suddenly they took out a big block and the reporter shouted in joy too. "Questo giorno rimarrà nelle memorie di tutti come quel giorno in cui l'unità dei popoli vinse sopra l'arroganza delle nazioni per restaurare la libertà e lasciar trionfare l'umanità. Un'umanità que non teme le barriere nè le muraglie." On November the 9th, 1989, the Berlin Wall fell, and Nicola had no idea why it was so important. One day the authorities had demolished a house a few blocks down, and they'd never talked about it on TV. Why all the fuss about this wall now?

- "Mamma? What's going on?"

Angela looked at him. All the anger was gone from her face. She suddenly looked much younger. Nicola realized she was beautiful. If he made an abstraction of the dirty apron, the messy hair and the tired eyes, Nicola could see a TV heroine dancing in the fountains of Rome and seducing Marcello Mastroiani.

- "Come here, *gioia mia*", she said tenderly.

She sat Nicola on her knees and patted his hair.

- "You know, *gioia mia*, there are a lot of conflicts on this planet. My *nonno* died in the Great War, a long time ago. And then your *nonno*, my dad, died in a war too. Another one. He died fighting for our freedom, you know. When that war ended, after a lot of people were hurt, everything changed. You couldn't recognize the good ones from the bad ones. You understand? So the Americans they saved us from bad people, but then they liked it so much, the fighting, that they looked for a new enemy to play at war with: the communists. But the new enemy was very strong and some people thought they were the good ones. Others said they were bad. And many said nothing because really, we did not understand much. So you know, sometimes one sees all these things happening and all these people being hurt, and you can't do anything. You're useless. It's like when Miss Marialisa explains a Math problem to you and she tells you that your answer is wrong. You feel powerless, right? You feel like others are telling you what to think and what to believe. You'll find a lot of that in life, *gioia mia*. Everywhere you'll find yourself trapped into following other people's orders and beliefs. Maybe you'll get tired and frustrated, just like me. Yet, I want you to be stronger than me, and to always remember that it doesn't always have to be like that. Many times you'll have to listen and do as other people say, but one day, when you believe in something strong enough, I want you to know that you have the power to change things too. Like those people standing on this wall. They refused to obey you see. They stood for what they believed in and they forced their government to listen. As long as I am on this earth, I will be your mother and you will have to listen to me and do as I say, you hear me? Because my only aim in life is your happiness. But nobody, not even me, can tell you what to feel, and what to believe in. You have to promise me that you won't end up like me, *gioia mia*! You have to promise me that you'll fight for your right to be happy and free! You understand?"

Angela had never talked to him like that. Ever. She was talking to him like to an adult, in a soft but firm voice. Nicola nodded, trying to remember everything she said because it sounded so important. He did not understand everything. He did not understand why she said she was frustrated. What did it mean? But he sure did understand he didn't have to believe Miss Marialisa when she'd say that subtractions didn't hurt anybody or that apples and oranges didn't belong together.

That night, Nicola couldn't fall asleep. He was trying to remember everything his mamma had said and write it on a piece of paper. For example, she had talked about his *nonno*, who had died in a war. She usually never talked about him. She never talked about the war either. Actually, Angela never talked about anything. Nicola had only ever seen his mum cook, gossip with the neighbors from the kitchen's window, or yell at him. That's why it was so important that he would remember every word. Suddenly, he heard the bang of the front door, then some muffled noises. He heard his mum shout and got scared. He did not know what to do. He wasn't supposed to be still awake at this time, so he didn't dare come out of his room. He stayed frozen in his bed, listening to every single noise, but they were too many of them, he couldn't follow. He heard shouts and grumbles. Sometimes it sounded like they were fighting, sometimes like they were having fun. After a while it all got quiet, and he fell asleep without even realizing.

* * *

The next morning Angela didn't look like herself. She didn't take him to school and was barely talking. She handed him a piece of bread then grabbed a trash bag and threw in all of Nicola's belongings.

- "What's going on, Mamma?"

She wouldn't answer. She finished packing, grabbed her son's tiny hand and pushed him out of the house. Nicola was scared and started resisting.

- "What are you doing, Mamma, where are we going?"
- "If people can tear down walls and defy an entire army to win their freedom, I sure can tear down that family and defy that father of yours!"

Then she fell silent again and walked down the street with a resolute look on her face. She looked up to all the women spying from their window and formed the sign of the cross on her chest. They all nodded and made the sign of the cross back at her. Resolutely, Angela grabbed Nicola's hand, and pulled him away.

They walked for a very long time. Angela knew she couldn't follow the main road, nor stop in any public place. Everybody knew who they were: Don Mario's wife and Don Mario's boy. They all had some sorts of debt with him. Don Mario had gained his position in the Fratellanza Napoletana, a cartel of camorrist families, by hooking up small business with cheap copies of pretty much anything. He had made some contacts in Albania… They'd ship him watches that looked like Rolex, or real Rolex that had "fallen out of the truck". Of course each shipment came with a bonus. At the beginning, the drugs were just for him, to earn the favors of his colleagues, or to bribe some cops here and there. Then the earth shook. The earth breached open in the middle of the night, literally and unexpectedly. Despite the buildings crumbling, despite the crushing darkness after the central electric tower had tilted, oscillated for a while, and finally crashed into the ground, despite the general chaos, everybody was standing in the street, petrified, watching Mount Vesuvio. The Vesuvio was trembling and growling. Heavy smoke rose up from his giant mouth. And while everybody was running, falling, and watching Mount Vesuvius, a group of Cutoliani (as they called those who followed Raffaele Cutolo) entered the prison hold of Poggioreale and coldly killed a whole bunch of "fratelli".

A couple of years earlier, Cutolo had earned the nickname of "O'Professore" in jail for being the only one capable of reading and writing. There, he rallied a bunch of camorristas to the idea that the Fratellanza Napoletana was led by old magnates who didn't understand the true potential of the organization. While the Cosa Nostra in Sicily was heavily armed and could rule over the whole island, the Camorra was limiting itself to petty thefts. Besides the lack of ambition, Cutolo also hated the lack of organization within the Camorra. Dozens of families shared the richness of the Campania. Each family controlled a territory as agreed through fragile pacts, which were regularly broken in the name of "vendetta". Cutolo envisioned a new organized institution, armed and more powerful than ever. He called it "La Nuova Camorra Organizzata": Nco.

After the killing on the night of the great earthquake, on November 23, 1980, Don Mario saw an opportunity he couldn't let go. He was handsome and smart (maybe those who knew him would rather say cunning). Mostly, he was famous for being ruthless. Handsome, smart and ruthless: there was little people wouldn't do for Don Mario. He knew how to convince them, how to use them, and he most certainly knew how to swindle them. He figured out who the killers were and went to see the "Generale", Pasquale Scotti, right arm of Cutolo.

- "Here's the deal, Generale. I can give the names of those scoundrels to my brothers and have them killed before sunset, or I can make sure nothing happens to them, and provide you with the best cocaine on this side of the Mediterranean. I might even give you good prices on the merchandise if you let me talk with some of your business owners. Simple and clean. So you can either enjoy a great trip to paradise, or buy your guys a ticket to the Russian mountains of pain."

Of course Angela didn't know the whole story. She only suspected that Mario was doing some shady business simply because in Naples, if you did well, you did wrong. Honest people in Naples never got rich, nor powerful. Honest people made *salsa di pomodoro*, they'd never see any borough other than their own and they'd die of old age surrounded by their family, without a sound, without having made a single wave in the great ocean of humanity. Angela was tired of being an honest person. Before she married Mario she had been beautiful and sexy, she had charmed many men with her self-confidence. When she was nineteen she had even lived a passionate romance with a young ebony prince from Morocco. She remembered the curve of his back, his behind round and firm like two apples. He treated her like a princess. One night he had surprised her with a Tagine: a Moroccan recipe learnt through generations of Bedouin mothers. She remembered the taste of the lamb, the strong citric pinch of the lemon, and the earthy taste of his fingers pressing the food in her mouth.

-   "Mamma, sono stanco! Nun voglio camminare chiu!"

She looked down to those big blue eyes looking at her.

-   "E cammini!" she ordered, angered as she wanted to keep reminiscing.

She needed to escape for a while, think so she could keep walking. She felt as if a hook could come grab her any second, pierce a hole in her heart and pull her back heartless yet alive to Don Mario. Nicola remained quiet resiliently and dedicated himself to keeping up to speed with his mum. She was going fast and his legs were still too short so he had to trot and grab her hand tight, anxious not to lose her. Angela was walking fast because she was angry, scared and anxious to leave the territories of the Camorra. As long as they were on Fratellanza ground, all she had to fear was people tattling. Most shop owners would not hesitate to give her up to Don Mario in exchange for a debt being forgotten. And all were in debt. Yet, they were now reaching the NCO territories, where things could easily get worse. Although the clans had not fought in nearly a year, she knew she still was an easy and desirable prey for ransom. Of course she had no idea that her husband actually held the whole city in his pocket, one half high on cocaine, and the other deep in debts and owed favors.

As she hastened her pace a bit more still, she started pondering where she was going. She had a cousin in Rome. Walking fast she'd get there in four or five days, but Nicola would never endure. On the other side, she was eager to leave the Campania region, where everything and everyone was somehow controlled by the Camorra. If she was running from her husband for intimate reasons, she was also running away from one of the Camorra's leaders. She suddenly realized she might not have properly considered how difficult and dangerous escaping would be. Panic exploded in her brain, ran down to her jaw which tightened up, gluing her teeth together, rushed like a waterfall down to her stomach which turned into a stone heavy like marble, pushing down her knees all the way to her feet which turned itchy like boiling olive oil. In a jiffy she slipped off her sandals, grabbed Nicola, sat him on her right hip, held her sandals in the left hand and started running. From that height, Nicola saw the streets of Naples end, the building turn into houses and the houses into rows of peach and lemon trees by thousands. He saw the sun rise to his midday position and slowly oscillate down towards the Vesuvius. Then he saw the Vesuvius grow smaller and smaller till it was just a hill like any other. He saw dogs running together with them for a while before they got bored, and cats mockingly yawning at them. Finally, they saw a white signpost that read *Napoli* with a big red line crossing it. As she saw it, Angela started slowing down and finally exhaled, breathing again. She got to the signpost, took one more step, checked that it was behind her for sure, and – at last – stopped running.

* * *

On the side of the small country road, Angela was laying down, her chest moving up and down with each huge breath she took. Nicola was looking at her, still dazed, still completely clueless, wondering if they'd ever go back, if he'd ever see his father again, and his friends, and Maestra Marialisa, or Beppe il Pizzaiolo. He placed his tiny hand on his mother's chest and felt the heart pumping fast. Angela pulled him down softly and invited him to lie down with her. There, in the middle of the peach trees, next to the big crossed signpost, Angela left behind her whole life. She left behind the *Quartieri Spagnoli* and its smells of *ragù* and oregano. She left the graves of her parents, the old women she used to help with their washing. She only took with her the joy of her life, her own creation: her baby boy. She looked at him and found in his big blue eyes the courage to stand up and keep going. They had to reach some sort of shelter before the night. She caught a couple of peaches, took Nicola's hand and pulled him through the trees.

They went on walking for three days, living on a couple of fruits Angela would reluctantly steal from some tree – not without reciting a prayer for forgiveness. On the first day they passed Caserta by the west, on the second day they fell asleep among the oranges of Camigliano, on the night of the third day they reached Marzanello. On that evening of mid-September, the last rays of light were fading out and Angela was still walking without an aim. Maybe they'd reach Rome, or at least she'd keep going while she had the strength. She looked at Nicola and was surprised to see tears running down his cheeks. She crouched down:

- "Why the tears, *gioia mia*?"
- "Devo far la pipì" sobbed the boy.
- "Why didn't you tell me you had to pee?"
- "You seemed angry, so I didn't want to make you even angrier."

Angela hugged him and realized she needed to find a solution to their situation pretty quick. They were passing by a village, composed of a hundred houses at most, all humble and tiny. Warily, she knocked on a door. An obese woman opened and looked at both of them with an investigating eye. Angela felt relieved when she guided them to the bathroom without a question. When they got out of the bathroom stall, they found *panini* ready for them. Mozzarella, prosciutto, and tomatoes in between two slices of home-made bread. Perfect! "Thank you, but we need to…" started Angela, but Nicola was already devouring a *panino* and flushing down a fresh orange juice. So Angela sat down. With every bite she felt her anger and despair fill her throat, flow up her mouth, heat up her cheeks. By the time she was done with her *panino*, she was sobbing and sniffing like a child. The big mamma – Maria - put a comforting hand on her shoulder and Angela let her tears flow out like a river. Maria took Nicola to the bedroom where he fell asleep at once, then returned to the kitchen and made coffee. The smell of the hot liquid tranquilized Angela a bit. Maria sat down in front of her and took her hand.

- "Vuoi parlarne, bimba?"
- "No."

Without a word, Maria disappeared in the bedroom. Angela looked around her trying to spot some sign of a man living here. The house was made of only two rooms: the kitchen and the bedroom. In the kitchen there were no pictures. There was a basket filled with wool on one side, and some kind of mannequin with pieces of cloth attached to it randomly. There was no sign of a masculine presence. Maria reappeared. She placed a little square of shiny paper in front of her. Angela took it and carefully unpacked it. She placed the piece of chocolate on her tongue and started chewing very slowly. She sat there, chewing in silence for about five minutes. Maria was cleaning the dishes letting time do its work.

- "I am running away. I have no idea where to. I took my baby boy and ran away from my husband. Now I don't know what to do."

Then she felt silent again. Years of gossips from window to window and from street to street had taught her that there was no hearing woman that could not talk.

* * *

The next day Angela woke up to find the kitchen table covered with little mounts of wool, each of a different color. Mamma Maria was agitating her needles in a joyful clicking.

- "Mi aiuti, bimba?"

Angela stood there for a minute, pondering what to do. Since she couldn't decide herself, she sat and did as ordered, following the instructions of Mamma Maria with some difficulty. A little after midday Maria sent her to pick some plum tomatoes, a bunch of zucchini flowers, and some *rucola*. Meanwhile Maria took Nicola to fetch the mozzarella. Nicola was observing. It was his first time away from home. Maria was getting desperate with Nicola stopping in front of every shop to observe the vendors and the assortment of sott'olii. Nicola had remained entranced with a couple of buffaloes quietly chewing on dry grass in their pen. He had been fed all his life with delicious creamy *mozzarella di buffala* but had never seen the buffaloes. They were heavy, their dark grey skin capturing the sun without keeping its heat, just like stones. They seemed so uncaring. Nicola was trying to reach them across the barrier with his tiny hand but they barely looked at him, gazing for a minute before returning to their chewing, indifferent to Nicola's waving. Nicola was considering how these big stone-like cows could give birth to something as light and heavenly as mozzarella. Maria read the surprise in his eyes. "Do you know how they do it, Nico?" Nicola shook his head with a look begging for explanations. She grabbed his hand and took him around the grange, behind the little shop, where a group of women was busy battering and mixing and filtering. They wore white blouses and blue paper on their shoes. They were singing about a lost love who had been taken by the winds of war and who should come back one day in search of the very best mozzarella in the country: that made by his beloved. Maria explained how the women woke up early in the morning to milk the female buffaloes. The milk came hot and smelly. They'd mix it with bacterial culture in huge wooden basins where it would sit for a little while, transforming into the *cagliata*. The women – dressed up in medical white blouses, their hair hidden under creamy hair nets, their muddy white clogs splish-splashing the wet floor – would soon start breaking the *cagliata* into smaller icebergs of coagulated cream. The tamed *cagliata* would then slowly sweat off its calcium, soaking for hours in maturation tubs.

In the next room, another team of nurses (as Nicola understood them) was massaging the mozzarella, tattering its flesh and pressing it gently to obtain the desired elasticity, transforming the magma into an incredibly soft-looking dough of the purest white.

- "Chisse è a Filatura" murmured Mamma Maria.

"The Filatura!" thought Nicola, giving to the word a whole new weight. He tried to pluck his index into the bath but Maria slapped his tiny hand before it reached the cream with the ability of a ninja.

- "Sii pazzo? E' acqua bollente, scemo!"

Nicola jumped a step back, suddenly afraid a splash of boiling water might reach him. Meanwhile, the nurses were disposing the non-spherical balls of cheese into long metallic basins where they'd harden up for a little while before undergoing the last process – the *Salatura* – where they'd get salted up in the most exact proportion to reach the most delicious combination of creaminess and saltiness on earth. One of the nurses saw the dribble running down the side of Nicola's chops. She grabbed a smaller ball and stuck it into the boy's mouth before Mamma Maria could see it. As Nicola plunged its teeth into the dough, the delicate skin of the cheese broke, giving way to a flow of milky water that tickled his taste buds like a hundred tiny mischievous imps. Nicola took his time masticating and chewing, making sure to forever engrave such incomparable taste of goodness on his memory.

It was already late when they got home. They found Angela in the kitchen, roasting the plum tomatoes in a pan. On the table, a plate of fried zucchini flowers was exhaling fumes of garden and olive oil. Nicola was disappointed he had missed the frying process. He loved it. He would always help his mother fill the flowers with cream cheese, then roll them in the flour before deposing them with delicacy into the pan where the olive oil would be crepitating in little bubbles exploding noisily yet softly. Still, he rushed to the table to devour a flower, crisp and soft, warm yet fresh when the cheese would touch the palate. Angela threw five handfuls of tagliatelle she had just made into the casserole of boiling water. The kitchen table was still patched with flour and little balls of dough. Nicola swiftly grabbed a couple and made them disappear in his mouth before Angela could see. Raw dough was his guilty pleasure. Angela would smash the wooden spoon on his hand if she saw him, yet Nicola would always take the risk. And Angela would always "forget" a few balls on the table.

The tagliatelle were now dancing in the water, jumping under the bubbles in harmony with the tomatoes shivering in their pan. It was as if pasta and tomatoes were talking to each other. Nicola often made up entire conversations between the two, sometimes very practical: "Isn't it hot in here Mr. Pomodor?" "Yes indeed Mrs Tagliatelle!", and sometimes rather philosophical: "What will become of us O Signor Pomodor? Will we ever be reunited? I am made of flour, eggs, and water. Yet, I am now something new that is neither flour nor egg nor water. Look at me, all tall and thin! But you, you were born tomato and will die tomato. They smash you and stir you, and you don't say nothing." Suddenly bubbles would burst from the sauce and Nicola would giggle. And Signor Pomodor responded: "Blub. Blub-blub. Don't you worry, bellezza mia! Soon we will be reunited. I am simmering with impatience!" Mrs Tagliatella would twist like a pretty ballerina inside her pot, urging Nicola to continue his prose. "For you, *vita mia*, I will transform into sugar, I will become the juice that exalts your delicacy." (He remembered how Mamma Maria had said that the salt exalted the delicacy of the mozzarella. He liked how that sounded more than he understood its meaning.) The mental conversation went on uninterrupted until

Nicola absorbed the last forchettata and buried the last of Signor Pomodor in his killer mouth.

* * *

The days passed by quietly in Mamma Maria's house. Angela would help sewing up doll clothes and cooking, while Nicola would learn the secrets of the origin of all things from Maria. Nicola was happy he didn't have to deal with mathematics anymore. He learnt how to grow carrots and eggplants and travelled around the area with Mamma Maria to sell them for a few *Lira*. Without realizing, Nicola was learning to add and subtract, replacing onions with money, and money with seed. When everything would be sold, Maria would give Nicola his part of the earnings, a few hundred *Lira* that Nicola would hide in his pants. In the evenings, Nicola would teach Mamma Maria how to read and write with an old copy of "I promessi sposi" di Manzoni, present from another era that reminded her that she once had a loving father who had hoped more for his daughter than this lonesome life. When he died in the Great War, she got rid of his clothes, his shaving tools, everything but this book that Nicola was now revealing to her, bits by bits, making her sob and sigh like a young girl.

Nicola felt happy in this eventless life. He barely ever thought of his father, whom he had not ever seen much anyway. One night, while sitting in bed, writing down a new story of his invention (since there were no books or TV for him to pass the time, he had taken on the habit of writing down his own stories, sometimes fantastic and magical, sometimes taken from his own reality), he overhead the voice of his mother through the thin wall separating the bedroom from the kitchen.

- "You know, the first time he beat me, I wasn't even surprised. I mean, I had married a handsome and powerful man. A mafia man. These kinds of men are no softies, that's for sure. Then it became a habit… he'd come home angry or nervous and I'd think "alright, he had a bad time, he might slap me around tonight but that's ok, that's how things are. Whenever he'd hit me, the next day he would show up with some flowers, or a new dress. When he'd beat me real hard, he would get himself forgiven with dinner out or some beautiful earrings. So I'd take the violence, and I'd take the presents. When I got pregnant, he stopped hurting me. On the contrary, he treated me like a queen. All the women in the *Quartieri Spagnoli* were jealous, so I'd invite them over to watch color TV or try on my jewels, and they'd love me. When Nicola started going to school, the violence came back. Worse. He'd come home drunk, or on drugs. I started paying attention to the way people were now talking to my husband. I had always seen a lot of respect in their eyes and that made me proud. My husband's power was my power! They loved him, and so they loved me. Then I started to notice that respect transformed into fear. People were making themselves small in front of him, like they were trying to disappear. He became a big shot, an arrogant brute! My husband had become a bad man, Maria. The more I realized how people feared him, the more I started fearing him too. The beatings became more frequent and I swear, Maria, I swear… I started hating him with all my heart. I want this man dead, Maria! Dead!"

She fell silent for a while, breathing heavily. Maria was standing behind her, a caring hand on her shoulder.

- "That night I decided it was the last beating I was taking from him, or from whoever" continued Angela. "When I saw those people pulling down that wall in Germany... you know, they showed it on the TV.... Some were even taking stones out with their bare hands, they were making holes in that wall and on the other side there were other people. People just like them. So I thought maybe if I tore down my wall I'd find people just like me too. Maybe I could do it too. Then he came home. He was drunk, or high, I don't know. He walked in direction of the room where my little boy was sleeping. He was going for him. I got so scared Maria! What if he were going to touch my boy? So I threw myself at him and tried punching him. He threw me on the floor. He was too strong. I was reaching for his face but all I managed to do was scratch him. So he said I should be glad he wasn't going to hit my pretty face. Instead he punched my stomach, again and again. He pulled up my skirt and forced his way in. I could feel his dick tearing my skin but all I could think of is that I shouldn't shout. I shouldn't wake up Nicola, my boy, my little boy shall never know what a bad man his dad is."

She felt silent again. She had stopped crying. She wasn't a woman any more, nor a wife. Now she was just a mother fighting for her son. From the bedroom, Nicola was listening. He was sitting with his back on the door, frozen. He was barely nine years old. He was a child. That day though, Nicola the dreamer died. Nicola the lamb who refused to harm with a subtraction, the bambino who ran after butterflies to discover where they were flying to… that boy died. On the same piece of paper where he had inscribed his mother's speech about choices and beliefs, he wrote in big printed letters:

V.E.N.D.E.T.T.A.

With that, Nicola promised himself that he would change things indeed. And if that meant killing his father, then that was exactly what he would do.

3- GAMES OF SEVEN ERRORS AND TIRED JOKES

Santiago, Chile, 1989

The broom wasn't there, where it was supposed to be. In its place stood the most frustrating nothingness. Juan tried not to panic. He might have got to the wrong house. They had moved here only a couple weeks ago after all. Maybe he just picked the wrong turn. He hunted around the block for his house. They all looked the same. Mud walls, corrugated iron roofs, tiny windows occulted with heavy black curtains. All of them held hidden something dangerous: a fugitive, weapons, Marx's communist manifesto, or more simply just a couple images of Allende and a K7 of Victor Jara. Five times he passed the broom-less house, five time he recognized the house – that one and not any other. He prayed for it all to be a mistake, a dream, a joke, something else than the only thing that the disappeared broom could mean. At first he prayed randomly "God, please, God, please, God-please, God-please!" By the third circle, the plea got more sophisticated. "Dear God, you know I don't particularly believe in you, but this is the time to prove you exist. Shazam, make the broom appear!"

By the time Juan had finished his fifth round, his prayers had grown into a bunch of curses and swearwords. He stood for a while in front of the door, unsure what to do next. He tried to peep through the windows but the curtains purposely unveiled nothing but the very image of the curious wanderer. An old woman passed by and looked straight into his anguished eyes. Juan tried to recompose himself and grumbled a hello – "Buenas, tía." She did not answer, but kept scanning him for a few seconds. She expressed her disapprobation with a gentle nod and went on her way, trotting sadly, chasing the walls as if to disappear in their shade, defeating the burning sun drumming on her back. For a moment Juan hesitated to ask her for help. If she had opened her mouth, if she had given him a sign, he probably would have, but she had left tormented by too many problems of her own already. Who had she lost? A son? A brother? Maybe even a grandson. Had he been killed, tortured, or was he one of those thousand who had been dragged into oblivion, and if so, was he alive or was he being eaten by the sharks alone in the ocean?

There was a guy who had stayed with them for a while, in the previous house, the one in Pudahuel. Juan quite liked him because unlike the other guests he never tried to "teach him about life, son". Sometimes he would even sit next to Juan and watch him build a tiny wooden house for the insects he had collected.

-   "See that spider? That's an Araña del Rincón. I found it there, in the ground where the others play soccer. It's deadly, you know? So that one I had to kill it. But I killed it with a needle so now I can still study it without it being all splashed down. Plus it's dangerous to smash them. If it bites you on the foot, for example, your skin will start dying all around the bite – that's called necrosis. If you don't cure it immediately, your cells will start dying inside. It will move along your veins and attack the liver. And then you die."

Pancho probably knew all of that already, but he would sit and listen to him all the same. He would even ask questions about other deadly spiders (Juan loved those) or about the proper nutritional regime for his colony of bugs – all carefully kept in little pots or improvised plastic cages. Then one day Pancho went out to a protest and never returned. Juan's father had waited a few days before writing down his name at the end of a long list of other names – a list he held in view of the day when everything would be over and somebody would have to remember. Somebody would have to denounce. The list bore no title, still everybody in the house knew very well what it was about: Los Desaparecidos. Dozens of names of men and women who had been taken by the militia and had never been returned to their family. Maybe they were held prisoners in the north, where the sun had burnt everything to a desert, or maybe they were floating at the bottom of the ocean, that angry Pacific Ocean which held so many secrets, serving the dictatorship like a faithful soldier: silent like Pinochet's secret police, ferocious like a hurt bulldog.

Sitting back against the faded amaranth wall of the opposite house, Juan was trying to think strategically and chase away that terrible conviction that his parents had been taken away. Were they being tortured, were they dead already? Would he have to add their names at the bottom of the list? Juan wanted to cry so badly. Him who always looked so tough and mature, he was now just a little boy, sitting in the dust, erasing away his tears. He had known the signal his whole life; it had always been the same. Still he recalled how his miniature mother had seemed so big and strong the day she had revealed the trick:

- "You see the broom outside against the door? That one is not to be touched, alright? It's our signal. You go through the door, you put the broom back in place, always! Every time you come home and you see the broom, you know it's safe to come in. You know everything is just fine. If one day you come home and the broom is not there, you do not get it in. Not for any reason. You hear me, son? If the broom isn't at the doorstep, you stay out, hidden, and wait. You wait for us to come home, *cachai*? "

It was on the morning of his third day in school that Mariana had given him the speech. Juan was barely five at the time, so the first two days she had walked him to the college in the morning, and back in the afternoon.

- "Here you turn right, remember, not the first turn, but the second one. Are you listening?"
- "Yes, mum!"

Juan was trotting along. Mariana always walked so fast. She hated being in one spot more than the necessary and always rushed from one place to the other, overlooking her shadow, making sure nobody was following. At every corner she would scan the street for armed forces before hazarding into the path, shaving the walls, hiding in their shade, like everybody else. Juan was not surprised by such behavior. That was the only way he had known his entire life. Walk fast, shave the walls, do not speak to anybody wearing a uniform! The uniforms were the absolute enemy. Heartless beasts.

That third morning she had woken him up a bit earlier than usual.

- "Time to be a big boy" summoned Mariana. ("A big boy? I'm five, what is she talking about?" Juan sure didn't like the sound of it.) "You remember the way to school, right? (unconvinced nod) Good. From now on you'll have to go to school alone, and come back home alone too. You understand, *cariño*? It's not far, you have to walk fast ("shave the walls, talk not to strangers... si si, I know Mama!") and do not stop in the way! You finish your classes, you come straight home. First I want to see you, then you can go and play with the others ("The others? What others? I never play with the others. They are mean and stupid!").

Indeed, Juan didn't have many friends. Probably, the fact that they changed neighborhood every six months or so didn't help much. At first he had been a very social kid, always running around, his little naked bottom bouncing from one game to the other. He'd share his toys (an iron tin, a piece of wool, an imaginary car) with the other kids of the block. Yet, by the fourth time they moved, Juan got tired of making efforts to bond with other children and preferred inventing worlds for himself. Since he had been taught about the broom and all the other "safety" rules, Juan had turned his world into a battlefield. All were potential enemies; no one was to be trusted.

Over the following four years, Juan learnt not only to find his way alone around perpetually new neighborhoods, but also to create universes for himself, worlds of magic and adventures. By the time he turned nine, he had already developed a strong sense of independence. On his own he took upon studying biology, mathematics, geometry. He'd capture all kind of bugs. Some he would dissect, learning to cut them in parts, leaving the head on one side (one), the legs on the other (two, three, four, five, six, seven), and the body alone (eight), exposed for Juan to explore it with its tiny wooden scalpels. And so he'd learn to divide, add and subtract. Only the multiplications resisted his logic. The biological world does not easily allow for multiplications, but Juan would deal. There were some bugs he wouldn't kill, but rather keep them alive and trap them inside little house he would build out of any material he could find. Plastic, wood, paper. He'd observe them and learn little by little what kind of food they liked. Sometimes he'd put two bugs together and one would eat the other. That was his favorite moment. See the nature in action. The big one eating the small one, without a single hint of pity, most naturally completing his reason-d'être, and introducing the weak to its fate and destiny.

Juan stood up. It was getting dark; he was hungry. He had to accept something had really gone wrong. He had an aunt about ten kilometers west. He could get there within two hours, but how? He had no idea how to get there, and no money for the bus.

He felt a presence behind him. Someone was following. He froze, trying to catch sight of the stalker with the corner of his eye, concentrating on noises and smells to detect a movement, a change. But he could hear nothing. Juan breathed deeply, relieved, and went on walking. But it started again. He could distinctively feel a presence. His legs started shaking but he refused to admit he was scared. He bit his lips, blew up his chest and turned at once, yelling like a lunatic: "Eeeeeeeehhh!"

The dog did not budge. It tilted its head to the right and look at Juan kindly. Juan let down his finger-gun and felt his heart beating again in his chest, together with a sudden urge to pee. "You scared me, dog!" and he pat him on the head. The dog licked his hand and made a couple turns on the spot, apparently chasing his own tail.

Juan felt a sudden exhaustion invade his body. He sat down, his cricket legs had gone numb. He curled into a ball. He had no strength left to fight the distress. Tears ran down his cheeks as his pressed his knees against his chest and tucked his face in. The dog laid down by his side and rested its head onto Juan's frail body as to cover him with its warmth. Slowly, sobbing and sniffing, Juan slipped into sleep.

Mariana and Manuel hurried up the street. The night had fallen, the lights were too dim. They felt their hearts pump strongly, beating with every step as they thought of their little one alone and scared in the dark night. They feared the police would never let them go. For four hours they had interrogated them. "Ignacio Saavedra. Who else was with him? We know he was planning an attack against our General. Who gave him the weapons? Who helped him?" They had arrested Pancho. Now they wanted names, more names. Despite the slaps and the beatings, Mariana and Manuel had kept silent. All they could think about was little Juan waiting for them outside of the broomless house.

Mariana found Juan huddled in between the murky wall and a flea-infested dog. Manuel bent over him and gently picked him up. He carried him to bed, careful not to wake him, but the rusty bed net squeaked pitilessly. Juan opened an eye and saw his daddy, a small scar still bleeding on his left cheek. He threw himself at him, circling his neck with his arms, hugging him with all his strengths till he could feel his heartbeat, till he knew for sure he was alive, there, with him, with him forever, forever and ever.

* * *

For the next five days Juan did not utter a word. He felt angry at the world, angry at the policemen who had left a big yellow and purple bruise on Mariana's back. He did not know how to express his pain and frustration. He felt that if he opened his mouth, it would be to shout so loud, so loud that it would break everything. The windows, the plates, the rules. But Juan was a good boy, incapable of violence. So he silenced himself and his rage. Even as Brazil scored its first goal, he repressed a moan of frustration and did not utter a world. The house was packed with people pushing and shoving, sometimes elbowing their way to the bathroom, causing everybody to complain. The bottles of beer would travel from hand to hand, soon followed by *Empanadas* filled with meat and onions, cooked by grouchy yet caring wives. By half-time, every man in the room was roaring his point-of-view on Orlando Aravena's strategy.

- "If I were the coach, I would send in Yañez and Zamorano to tackle Brazil from both sides, giving room for Basay to move in and bam, goal compañeros! Goal!"

The second half started with everybody in every house of Chile shouting "Chi-Chi-Chil, Le-Le-Le, viva Chile!" a litany that reverberated against every wall to fill up the air with hope and relief. Chile would classify for the Italy 1990 Mundial, and it would go as a democracy, a Republic led by a legally elected President. Sure the country was still divided, sure armed policemen were still taking people away and all those who had resisted all these years had yet to see something change for them, but if Chile was to go to Italy, then everything would be possible. Then Juan and his family could return to live normally in a country known for its grandeur, not for its thousands of *desaparecidos.*

Juan was following the game with the uttermost concentration, praying with all its strength for Chile to win. Brazil was leading by one goal, but everything was still doable. Suddenly, out of the blue, a sparkler flew over the field, knocking down Chile's beloved goalkeeper. Everybody held their breath as they watched Roberto "Condor" Rojas fall down to the floor, rolling from side to side, blood running down his forehead, the rest of the team buzzing around him like an army of disoriented bees. In the middle of the all-Brazilian crowd's boos, the players were raising their hands, hassling the referee, some even giving the finger to the hissing spectators. Those watching, glued in front of their TV screen, or listening from their transistors all over Chile were still keeping religiously silent, waiting to see what would happen. As they announced that the Chilean team was abandoning the game claiming conditions to be too unsafe, everybody broke into a moan of protest, some even throwing their glass against the wall (not in Juan's house, though, they could not afford to break anything at all really). The chaos generated by the incident continued for a good half an hour as Rojas was taken away by the medical team, the Chilean players were accusing Brazil of trying to kill them, the police interrogating the some one hundred and thirty thousand supporters hosted by the Maracaná stadium, the radio speakers exhorting the culprit to come clean, and the Brazilian players still sitting in the grass waiting to know if they could go home as winners – or what?

The whole thing was starting to become slightly funny when the commentator announced the official victory of Brazil by one to zero, and therefore the elimination of Chile from the Mundial. The long faces around the transistor were not expressing even half of what Juan was feeling. Chile wouldn't go to Italy, Chile would remain a bleeding torn up country, and he would remain a lonely child constantly preoccupied with the disappearance of people and things.

In the middle of the gloominess, Manuel raised an authoritative index, and declared:

- "We may have lost the game, but we haven't lost our dignity. We are fighters. Seventeen years we have resisted! Seventeen years we have shown those fascist dogs that they could jail us, torture us, silence us, but they could never break us. There are only three months left before the presidential elections. Our time has come. Our time has come to reclaim what is ours: our freedom! Allende is not dead *hermanos*! Allende lives on as long as his ideals live on, through us, through our martyrs, and through our companions all over the world!"

His last words were followed by a roar of the twenty-two men jammed up in between the bathroom door, the kitchenette and the small table where stood the transistor, three empty beer bottles, and a leftover *completo* – a rachitic sausage and a hint of avocado barely sticking out from the bread.

That was Manuel's talent. He could exhort the crowds, cheer up his boys with his grand speeches, and shut anybody up with a single movement of his right eyebrow. He was the one heating up the spirits one minute, and calming everybody down the next. Right now all were hugging and superbly declaring what each one would do with Pinochet's body after he was officially taken down.

Everybody had already forgotten about the game but Juan, who was still kneeling by the table, his ear stuck to the crepitating speaker of the transistor.

- "Shhhhhhhsh!" Then louder: "Shush you all!"

The men looked at him bewildered. The boy was talking! Juan pumped up the volume revealing the squeaking voice of the commentator who suddenly had gone from tenor to soprano in less than a second.

- "Joao Havelange, estimadisimo FIFA President, has come down to the tribune where our special forces have arrested the alleged flare thrower! Wait, they are taking the culprit away. It is unbelievable, ladies and gentlemen. As I speak I cannot believe my eyes: it's a woman! A woman indeed who has savagely attacked our beloved Cóndor, our hero of the Chilean selection! For our listeners on the radio who cannot – unfortunately – enjoy the whole show, let me describe to you the woman who is now being taken away by this very efficient Brazilian police (a model of order and efficiency, really!). She is blond my lords, oh yes she is! A tall Brazilian woman in all her splendor. We have not received any information as of yet as to why she threw the sparkler straight at Rojas, but we all know how those things go, don't we? Am I sensing a love affair gone wrong? It seems that our best goalkeeper of all time is also a dangerous Don Juan!"

Juan jumped. He did not like at all hearing his name associated to this whole situation.

- "Ladies and gentlemen, incredible, the giant screen is now revealing the footage of the incident. The crowd has gone wild, nobody understand what's going on… No! I cannot believe my own eyes, this can't be happening! Ladies and gentlemen, the head of security is now reporting the results of the analysis of the footage and it seems that Rojas was never actually hit by the flare! We are watching the images right now and – indeed – this is unseen, this is incomprehensible, it seems Rojas was never hurt by the flare but by himself! It seems, my dear listeners, our Condor has ceased to fly and has sold himself to Brazil, betraying not only his team, but the whole of Chile. But wait, here comes an announcement…"

The commentator went silent after bursting uninterruptedly for about five minutes. In the back they could hear a voice on the big stadium speakers announcing something unintelligible in Portuguese. Everybody waited, they had forgotten to breathe, those who previously were in line for the bathroom had now forgotten they even had to go; even the women were listening carefully, peeping in from the back door. The voice stopped speaking and was followed by what could be recognized as extreme agitation in the backward. The commentator let a few more seconds pass before he managed to mouth, slowly, a translation of the announcement.

-   "Due to alleged corruption and a tentative to invalidate the game on the part of the Chilean team, the FIFA is automatically disqualifying the Chilean team from both the 1990 and 1994 World Cups."

* * *

It was all over. Chile was disqualified. And not only there on the field. Together with its soccer team, the whole of Chile was feeling disqualified and hopeless. On December 14, 1989, Chileans of all shapes and colors came down to vote. Pinochet had already been voted out by 55.99 points. Now they were lining up, suspicious and frustrated, to elect the new President of the Republic of Chile. Büchi, Errázuriz, or Aylwin? There was nobody to vote for.

- "All of 'em rich dogs who've never held dirt in their hand. Quikos all of 'em!" would spit Manuel. "Don´t get your hopes up, compadres! They´re just serving the same tasteless dish on a different plate."

Juan was standing in line, dangling from his father's hand, observing the women's row on the opposite side of the school's yard. There were heavy ones, packed down like canvas bags standing on reversed ice-cream cones. Others were all voluptuous curves, with long dark hair brushing their hips. Whistles and blown kisses would erupt from every other line, each young bloke trying to attract the attention of one or another.

- "Uy compadre! Mira esa chiquilla allá! Ella, chascona con el vestidito rosado!"
- "Manu, what's your favorite, huh?"

They all tried to get Manuel to joke around with them, reveal some secret crush. But Manuel only had eyes for Mariana. She had been his muse since the first time he had seen her at the post office. She wore a bright fuchsia dress and a shawl painted in large green and red flowers. She'd always correct him:

- "They were turquoise and amaranth red, *amor*! If you're gonna tell the story, then tell it right, *poh*."
- "*Mi vida*! You know I don´t see the difference. There's red, there's blue, and there's yellow. Everything else looks just the same to me."
- "*Ay por Dios*! Twenty years together and only now do I realize I married a blind fool!"

And she'd give him a loud kiss on the cheek, pouting with her lips yet laughing with her eyes.

- "Juan! Stop picking your nose!"

Juan jumped, startled, and hid a booger behind his back, rolling it away in between his thumb and index. Manuel pulled him forward. The line was moving way too slow. Juan wanted to go back to his games. Especially since he had a new friend to play with: a leafy cricket Juan had found early in the morning just a couple days earlier. That one was fun so Juan did not want to dissect it. Instead he built a special house for him with a tall glass bottle he had stolen from a neighbor. The cricket would jump around tirelessly, and Juan would spend hours observing it soar up, trying to catch the movement of the legs, fixing it in his mind and replaying it like a slow motion movie. The line was advancing a couple centimeters every ten minutes and Juan was dreaming of the cricket bouncing up and down in his bottle. He recalled the muscles, the clicking out of the knee, and the extension of the body.

Finally they got to the polling table. Mariana had already voted at table 68 – the women's table. They were far less women queuing, for some reason. Manuel crushed his thumb into the blue inkpad, and then pressed it against the white paper board, next to the name Francisco Javier Errázuriz Talavera from the Progressive Union for the Centrist Center.

- "What else can I do, son? It's the least rightist of all three…"

That evening rightists, leftists, communists, pinochetists, men, women, hoping or fearing, praying or cursing, all were reunited again, some in front of their fancy color TVs, others jammed up around their half-broken transistors. Juan was sitting in the back on top of the last crate of ammunitions. Pinochet had renounced office over a year earlier, accepting the ruling of the Chilean people, yet nobody in the front believed him. Not only Pinochet was very unlikely to leave, he was also expected to retaliate. So Manuel and the other *frentistas* all kept their guards up. The war had not ended yet, and if it were to last another ten years, then they would fight another ten years, or however much more they had to. They had not fought for sixteen years to see their sacrifice go to ruins. Besides, what else could they do? You don't live in secret, plagued by fear, obsessed only with fighting and surviving, and then go back to an office job as if nothing had happened, do you? At only nine, Juan was chewing on the same dilemma. All his life he had been in the resistance. He had learned how to throw a punch at six, and how to shoot a weapon at eight. So? What next? How do you fight a make-believe democracy?

Meanwhile a soft lady voice was keeping the country updated on the results. The numbers were growing bigger and already Aylwin was far ahead. The counting went on for hours. Reporters would invariably fill the wait with similar stories across Santiago: all were listening and waiting; all were bored.

Finally, only a few minutes before midnight, the last of the bulletins were recollected and the results came out, officially. Aylwin was the winner. Aylwin who was "a nobody, a puppet, a stupid dog panting cowardly at his master!" roared Manuel, only expressing the common sentiment in the room. Only a few minutes later, Pinochet's voice resonated all over Chile.

- "Chilenos y Chilenas. I am most happy to cede the honor of leading this great country to such a great man. Nevertheless, I cannot abandon my people and I must ensure the security of this nation. This is why, together with Aylwin and members of the Congress, we have agreed that I would stay as Commander in Chief of the Army, thus ensuring the safety and wellbeing of my country."

Everybody fell quiet. The room was as packed as on soccer days, yet you could hear a fly's buzz. They all went home, without a word. There was nothing to say. Chile was not going to Italy. Chile was not going anywhere at all. Of course they knew nothing was to change. They didn't expect *Pinocho* to give up power, yet they had hoped. Foolishly, childishly, they had hoped.

Everyone returned to the darkness of their home, the dust on their clothes had invaded their heart. They felt immensely tired. Tomorrow they'd see what to do about it, but not tonight.°

Tonight was for sleeping. Tonight was for dreaming.

2002

4- OTTOMANS AND OTHER PEOPLE WITH BIG NOSES

Washington D.C., USA, 2002

- "Ottomans invented ze wine!"
- "Ahah! What are you talking about? Romanians invented wine of course! And computers! And what did Pashtun people invented Sameer?"
- "Huummm… cocaine and resistance!"
- "Wahahaha! Ottomans invented resistance, man!"

Sameer loved that scene repeated over and over again. Anor would always argue that Ottomans invented pretty much everything, then Turks sold the patent rights to the *damn Americans*. By his side, Adrian – forever sweeping a glass of wine –, overlooking the room from behind the bar, the soft lights giving the whole scene a Kusturica vibe. Anor was talking in his heavy accent, pointing at him while the smoke of his cigarette was taking over his fingers. This was his favorite moment; it felt like being part of a movie, maybe Camarón de la Isla would come in through the door, everything would turn black and white, a beautiful woman dark eyes and scarlet lips would come ask him for a cigarette... Fellini meets Kusturica.

Sameer had just finished his shift. One of his tables was still sitting in a booth, sipping on their wine. The fat guy talking loudly had ordered one of the most expensive bottles on the menu to impress the ladies: a Duca Enrico Reserva 1995, 100% Nero d'Avola. Italian wine at its best. He had popped the cork with the reverence due to such delicacy, versed it in the decanter, let the peppery aromas fill his nostrils. He had never been to Italy, yet he already knew all about its ground, its herbs, the heavy hands of the man who had picked the grapes. A wine like that – if listened to – could tell you about all the love stories and all the dramas of Sicily. A man crying over a treacherous woman. The latter hiding amongst the grapevines with a letter from her lover. The lover being killed in a duel against the husband. Sameer had a very romantic conception of Italy....

Deaf to the dramatic stories of duels and deaths, the fat guy had smelled it, agitated it, tested it, spitted it, and complacently announced:

- "This wine is corked, young man! Why don't you bring me this little Chianti of yours instead?"

Don't ask me twice, thought Sameer. And off you go, the Duca Enrico hidden in the back.

- "Don't worry, we'll take care of it later" had said Nori with a wink.

Nori was the sweetest woman. She had bought the restaurant together with her brother a few years before, from an old couple of Piedmontese who had decided to return to their homeland after 50 years of exile. Together they redecorated the place, being cooks, waiters, and managers all at once - till they could start hiring. Together they built the first organic restaurant in DC; all fresh food and northern Italian cuisine. On the red walls, they had left hanging years of fanatic memories: pictures, shirts, helmets, even a full bicycle which once belonged to the famous Italian cyclist, Fausto Coppi... or so ran the story. One of the pictures in black and white showed Coppi after winning the Tour de France for the second time, a ravishing woman in his arms. The whole thing looked so glamorous, so elegant, so... well, Italian.

Coppi's organic restaurant was born and filled little by little with friends and grateful strangers. Nori's passion for music soon attracted musicians and dancers into the place. By 2001, it had become the late-night go-to place for the whole of DC's Flamenco crowd.

Yo me encuentro triste y solo

Y buscando por la calle

Mi camino

Porque soy un vagabundo

En mi tierra, en el mundo

Mi Camino

Yo me encuentro triste y solo

Y buscando por la calle

Mi camino

El camino, mi camino

El camino del verano

Y yo soy un vagabundo

Yo me voy por este mundo

Mi guitarra entre las manos

Tocando por mis hermanos

El camino

La mujer que yo más quiero

Es la que me sigue fiero

El camino

Yo la quiero tanto tanto

Y por ella canto canto

El camino

Mi guitarra entre las manos

Tocando por mis hermanos

El camino

El camino, mi camino

El camino del verano

Perched on his bar stool, a glass of exquisite wine on one hand and a cigarette on the other, Sameer let his thoughts navigate through the music. Somehow, the nostalgia of the music brought him back to his first moments in the United States of America. After the Russians had gone and the Talibans had taken over, after the repression had crumbled down all hopes of return to Afghanistan, his father had started thinking that maybe things were not going to get better any time soon. One day he went down to Peshawar, and started waiting in line in front of the US embassy. After three hours of pacing, he had shared his whole life story with a number of fellow applicants.

- "Don't even bother with a visa, uncle! I have been waiting three years and nothing happens. What? Do you think they care about us over there? They are all busy driving around in their giant cars and selling their wives like prostitutes."
- "And eating dirty pigs" added another.
- "It's true, and they all look like big fat pigs too, but they are helping us against the Russians!" continued another three rows down the line.
- "Oh common Khalel, the pigs don't help nobody but themselves! - Listen to me son…"

Hamid Ahmadi turned to look at the old man who was now talking to him: the face of a hawk, one tooth, one leg, one huge nose.

- "You've got better chances applying for the green card than for a visa… and that gives you about… one chance in a million!"

The man exploded in a laughter bigger than himself and added "Good luck, son" tapping on his shoulder repeatedly and laughing compulsively.

-   "The grinkart?" Hamid repeated.
-   "The grriiiiin-karrrD, my son! You gotta look for the grriiiin-karrrD-lotttari!"

* * *

- "Good morning, auntie. I want to apply for the grinkardlotari."

He had pronounced it all in one breath so much the woman in front was having him confused and impressed. She was neither big, nor fat, and she sure didn't look like a pig. No-no... she looked more like a bird, a swan for example. Hamid Ahmadi had seen swans once in an illustrated book. They were gracious and white, very white, with a tall neck. She was just like that.

- "You mean the gwiin-kad-lott'wi, sir?"

Hamid listened to those weird sounds and inspected her mouth searching what she was chewing on. He saw nothing so he simply concluded she was an angel and was chewing on a piece of heaven. He had accepted to consider moving to America only very reluctantly, only after he finally accepted the evidence: if he wanted to keep his children safe and free, he could never return to Afghanistan. The too many stories of assassinations and mutilations carried out by Talibans had crushed his last hopes of ever meditating at his parents' grave again. He thought he would go to America only to save his children and send money home till the conflict was over, but now he was starting to think that maybe they could actually be happy there, and live in a big house and have one of those giant cars. He could offer his wife beautiful white dresses so that she could look just like a swan too.

- "Sir? Here's the form, sir. You need to fill it and send it over to this address by November 2. It is in English though. Do you speak English?"

He nodded his head "Kha, kha… huu… Yes! Yes!"

Just as he got down the bus back to Chargulli, Hamid started running. All day he had been carrying in his heart, in his whole body, an anxiety that made him feel ticklish. He wanted to run and jump and pray God to send him to the swan-filled America. He was already dreaming of his life over there.

- "Son! Son! You gotta help me… we're going to Amriki Insh'allah!"

Over the notes of the guitar flamenca, Sameer could still hear the scritchiscratch of his pen conscientiously writing down P-A-K-I-S-T-A-N under "country of origin", the contestations of his mother who didn't like the swan-lady story at all, the laughter of his smaller sister singing "mong da Amrika lamoo, mong da Amrika lamoo!". And then, there had been the waiting. For months and months. Till everybody nearly forgot about it. Then a letter: Yes! It was a yes! There'd been a lot of shouting and crying of joy, a lot of food, and a lot of dreaming. Then a lot more waiting at the Embassy, the swan-lady had gone, replaced by a tall black guy who spoke Pashto like a Russian cow. Then a lot more trips to Peshawar to fill in one more document still, to get yet another certificate. More waiting, another letter, more yelling, more food, a lot of questions too. To start with, who will go with the patriarch? The paper said just him and a direct familiar. It would be Sameer. He was old enough and could help bring in money with his hard work. Sameer, who had not been asked anything, was sitting in silence turning the idea around in his head. "America! It's damn America! I mean it's crazy out there, right?"

Sameer had thought of the friends he would have been leaving behind, his town, his land. He felt that going was like betraying his people, abandoning the others to fight and fulfill his own duty. Then he had thought of what the United States must have been like. In all the action movies he had watched with Najib and Qasim, there were always big buildings, very strong black men, and super-hot women wearing leather jackets and flashing their hair around. Sameer was fifteen years old then and he was finding himself paying way too much attention to women. Just earlier that morning, him and the boys had remained slightly aroused from the sight of a group of young women passing by them. They had tight *salwars* revealing nothing more than a juicy slice of ankle, and a lot of *khol* around the eyes. They looked like those *Pollywood* (a much worse Pakistani equivalent to Bollywood) heroines on posters and TV ads, with giant bosoms and exaggerated make-up. The guys never managed to finish one of those cheap movies so filled with romance and drama. Plus the heroines were fat and wore tight spandex under their sari-like *qamees*. They displayed ecstatic smiles which they kept even while singing of their pain due to their uncompromising parents who refused to give their daughter to a man of lesser conditions (who invariably carried a bushy beard and a funny haircut). Rather than drama and love, the boys preferred the fights and the guns. They usually watched Indian action movies with lots of visual effects, men throwing punches at each other and swirling around in the air before falling heavily in a magnetic *thump*. Lately though, Sameer had started to wonder what women looked like below their *salwars* and how it would feel to touch their skin.

While his parents were still discussing over the details of the trip, devising a thousand different scenarios, mostly arguing about the dangers of a depraved society with such different values, Sameer had swooped out of the house to meet Najib and Qasim. Of course, they had heard of the big news. The whole town had heard of the big news! They had talked for a while about how awesome it was that he could go to America. Then they had joked about what he would have done there, and all the cool stuff he would have gotten to do. Like watch TV when he wanted, and look at girls, or eat at Makdonalad and drink tons of Kuka Kula. And meet girls. Girls… One look at each other had sufficed to know their minds had met: Qasim's cousin's ultra-secret movie rental!

That day was, indeed, the perfect occasion to try a new genre Najib had heard about from his older brother – one that they knew could get them in huge trouble if ever caught watching it: the American productions… or as authorities called them, the "porno" movies.

- "We want to see naked girls."

The single-toothed guy behind the counter had inspected them with a dubious eye. Even though watching movies was allowed by authorities back then, mullahs strongly discouraged their consumption. Therefore, rental stores were secret palaces hidden in the backyard of some daring investors. Everybody watched TV or movies, but nobody talked about it by fear of reprimands from the mullahs. And even between religious leaders there were strong disagreements. There were the progressive mullahs, who followed the Qur'an. They only prohibited depictions of the prophets and left open the way to painters and miniaturists to color this world with delicate figures and tiny faces. And there were the orthodox mullahs, who followed the Sunna, secondary source of the *shari'a* Islamic law, and recited it with a finger raised to intimate fear and respect, "Whoever makes a picture, Allah shall torture him with it on the Day of Judgment until he can breathe life into it, knowing he will never be able to."

Sameer's very religious aunt had taught him those severe ahadith, which had shocked the boy to the point he still could hear her firm voice scanting those words like a threat. Most of Pakistan, though, was educated on the Qur'an alone, and pictures and movies abounded in the undergrounds of any shop tender with a progressive fiber. And there was music too, which Sameer was particularly keen on. Sometimes, he would sit in the dirt on the riverbanks and listen to a decrepitated old Sufi – thin as a twig – but with a voice so ethereal and so vibrant that even donkeys would stop and listen to his call. He would enter in a direct dialogue with God, an ancestral chant of poetry and music called Qawwali. Najib's grand-father would often join in and play the harmonium, while youngsters would bring in a *rebab* or a tabla. Others would start swirling their head around in an obsessive back-and-forth movement. As the music brew, they would stand up and bring their whole body into movement, turning around, throwing their long black hair backward in an entranced imitation of the century-old Attan dance… the traditional swords being replaced with dusty handkerchiefs, the slashing of the blades with handclaps. Sameer would try the steps sometimes, but he was much better at singing. He would repeat the words of Nusrat Fateh Ali Khan.

MaiN azal se bandaa-e-ishq huuN

muhhe zuhd-o-kufr kaa Gham nahiiN

mere sar ko dar teraa mil gayaa

mujhe ab talaash-e-haram nahiiN.

I am a follower of love since the beginning of my life,

I do not care for piousness or irreligiousness.

My head has found your house,

Now I do not search for the mosque.

Sameer kept chasing the melody away from his thoughts as he concentrated to remember every detail of that far away night of 1994, when he had stood in that rental store, begging the pondering video vendor. After infinite supplicating from the boys, the rascal had finally given in and handled them an obscure American movie, with a dog and a blond girl on the cover. Najib had quickly hidden the booty in his *chader*. Qasim had thrown a few rupees on the counters and off they'd gone, like criminals hiding a dead body, razing the walls and watching out for wandering policemen. If caught – they knew – those corrupted representatives of the law would have made them pay till their last rupee in exchange for their silence. Without the appropriate bribe, they would have told their little secret to the whole district, bestowing upon the boys shame and embarrassment. For a porno movie, the price for silence would be even higher… Hence, they had to be very quiet, and very very discreet.

The night had fallen. They had run through the darkest allies, carrying a whole bunch of VHS tapes, a TV set and a dirty VCR covered in stickers. They had arrived just in time to set up their material in the *hujra* before rejoining their respective family for dinner – displaying the most innocent faces and proudly announcing "I was playing soccer with the guys… I'm so hungry now!"

After a delicious *potah* of potatoes, tomatoes and chicken livers, Sameer had rushed out of the family room, back to the *hujra* where his partners in crime were already waiting for him, distended on large pillows, their cheeks red with anticipation. The movie was plain stupid but the boys did not care about the story. There was a dog that was kind of smart, and policemen, and heavy suspense music… but what had captured the guys' attention was the images of cities where Qasim and Najib would never get to go, with glass buildings and wide paved streets. The girls wore short skirts revealing more legs than they had ever seen. Their 80s' style T-shirts fell loose on their snow-white shoulders, and they all had sun glasses that made them look very cool and fashionable. Then there had been The Scene! That one passage in the movie that the gang would never forget: the shower scene! She was tall and blond and she entered the shower naked. The camera first showed her naked back, then she turned around – oh so casually –, the water dripping from her hair, along her cheeks, along her shoulders, down to her tender round breasts that were now directly exposed for full enjoyment to the viewers. Their first breasts ever! Najib was sitting down in ecstasy, eyes wide open, drawling. Qasim was holding the remote control and hitting the review button every time the scene came to an end, each time wiggling and exhilarating. Sameer was keeping quiet. He had been trying to control the urgent need he'd felt to reach for his trousers, untie, and touch himself right there where it tingled and burnt. A bump was showing which he was trying to cover with his *qamees*. It felt like his whole body was itching and he wanted to rub himself very hard and let it all out. Then he had thought about his mum and wondered if his mother's breasts looked the same. Suddenly, out of nowhere, the itching was gone and so was the bump in his trousers.

* * *

The next thing Sameer remembered was seeing vast forests and little white houses from a thousand meters above. Through the plane's window, Sameer had scanned the landscape looking for the tall skyscrapers he had seen in the movies, trying to spot the capitol and the White House. All he could see were green spots and little white dots with little blue squares on the side. Maybe he had been disappointed, or released. He couldn't say for sure. Nearly seven years after his landing on the US soil, Sameer had learned to love the small houses. In the first few years, he had lived in a typical townhouse in Alexandria. It was made of well-ordered red bricks and had a basement that Sameer and his dad were sharing. To get in, you had to go down a few white stairs. It was all so clean and perfect that it didn't look real till you'd get inside. Then it was just a room with nothing inside. The nothingness made the room look gigantic, bigger than their whole house in Chargulli.

Little by little they'd managed to buy a mattress, a chair. Sometimes the owners who lived upstairs would let them use the kitchen but mostly they would only cook just one thing: chicken karahi. It helped them feel at home for a while. They would always invite the landlords to share their meal. The first time they accepted, afterwards they would always refuse politely. They'd both concluded it was because of the spices. Americans had fragile stomachs. It had made them both laugh out loud. Nowadays, Sameer realized maybe it was something else too.

Eventually his mum and siblings were able to join them. Sameer was making decent money working in a Spanish restaurant after school. He would do everything, from washing dishes and chopping onions to waiting tables. Soon, they all moved into one of those white suburban houses he had first spotted at his arrival. It was so big that it had three rooms only to sleep and an entire room dedicated just to sitting and watching TV. For his parents, who had lived their whole life discussing – arguing, rather – the news over sand, dust, and sweat, for them world news had nothing to do with suits, ties, sofa, and A.C. Ha! A.C. The flamenco music was leading Sameer into a weird trip down memory lane. Air Conditioning had been quite a theme with the women of the family. Hamid wouldn't pretend to put it on, arguing that they never had it in Pakistan so why surrender now to an apparatus that cost them money, was not officially approved by the mullahs, and had them live in damn Russia all year long. "Tell that to my menopause!" had shouted Shazmina. Hamid had stood there for about five seconds before he could make any sound or movement. Never! Never ever had he heard a woman, not even his own, talk about intimate matters. Periods, hot flashes, shaving creams and lubricants were of those topics you just did not talk about. While everybody was still there, standing, not knowing what to say, Shazmina grabbed a post it and stuck it on the AC box. It read "No touch".

There were very few occasions Shazmina would get really angry or go against her husband's will. The AC was one; the day Sameer announced his desire to leave the house was another. That second one, though, couldn't be solved with a post-it.

On New Year's day of the year 2000, Sameer decided that a new millennium and being twenty were two good-enough reasons to go and live on his own. Since his arrival in the US in 1995, he had done nothing but the school-work-bed routine. Only on Sundays did he have some time to hang out with his friends. Because he didn't drink alcohol, eat pork, or party all night long, Sameer had had a hard time binding with the locals. In Chargulli, Sameer never had to worry about making friends. Qasim and Najib had been his friends since as long as he could recall and they did not need any alcohol, hot wings, or loud music to "get going" as Yankees said. Building a friendship with a local was such a foreign ritual to him that, despite its best efforts to blend in, all of his friends were Pakistani. His two best friends were even from the same area of Northern Pakistan. Roshan was as dark as a moonless night and as skinny as a street dog. The guys made jokes about it, especially since his name actually meant "clear" or "bright". So they'd nickname him Taarh Spey – which meant dark dog – or sometimes just Neswarey - brown. Just as Roshan was the new Najib, Khalil may have been the new Qasim. Just like him, he wasn't very smart but he always knew where to find the good stuff. Once in a while, he'd bring the best *naan* bread in town, some other time he'd uncover the purest stash of Marijuana. The three would inhale the smell of weed, one by one, before smoking it. More than the high it provided, the three loved how it reminded them of home. Even though Islam prohibited its consumption, it was very common for Pashtu men to smoke it. The older they'd get, the more they'd smoke. "Who the hell knew what was legal or illegal in Pakistan anyway?" they'd retort to the evil-saying. And Khalil would shout with joy "Who the hell knows what's legal and what's illegal in the US anyway?" and they'd all laugh, exalted by the drug, nostalgia, and the feeling of doing something dangerously illegal.

- "How about another beer, Sameer? The night is young; it's time to see you dance!"

Anor's voice brought him back to reality. He ordered another Moretti Rossa, lit another cigarette, and watched Cesar play a Buleria with the ease and delicacy that was his. Sameer suddenly realized that sitting in the booth by the door were the Gypsies. He smiled. He knew the night was only starting and he knew the show would be good. The presence of the Gypsies also gave him a little more time to reminisce. The night wouldn't die young, that was for sure! Sameer wanted to go back to that time it all had really begun for him. That day he left home and his life in the suburbs, and with it everything that made him a true Pathan. That day he became a Pakistani-born American, that day he acknowledged officially that from now on his life would take place in the United States of America and that he would act accordingly.

Of course he had felt a knot in his stomach as he had pronounced those words:

- "Baba, mama, I am twenty now, the new Millennium has come, nothing happened, we've been living here five years and it has become clear that we're not going back to Pakistan. So I've decided to give myself a chance in this country."

Shazmina had stared at him with her eyebrows brought together. It had taken him a few seconds to find the energy to declare:

- "Baba, mama, I'm going to live in DC. On my own."

Shazmina had looked at Hamid, Hamid had looked at Shazmina – it was understood. This one was of those few occasions when Hamid let Shazmina do the talk.

- "Ma bashey, you think you're American now, huh? You've just become like them, individualist, thinking you're too good to live with your parents!"
- "Mum, I don't think that, I just want to try live my own life. And, you know, I work in DC now. It's not convenient for me to keep commuting for two hours every day."
- "You don't love me!"
- "Of course I do, even if I move to DC, I love you just the same." (*Allah don't let me down!* shouted Sameer in his mind.)
- "Fine! You wanna go and live in the city with the white people and forget all about us, go! Go, then!"

Damn! Shazmina had a talent for leaving people on mute! "Seriously? That's it?" thought Sameer. He should have known better; he should have suspected something. But youth is arrogant and likes to think they are on top of it all. So he declared victory, found himself a hero, although he did give some credit to the half-moon. Deep down his guts had told him that something was going on, but he'd chased the thought away because all hell were lose, he had won the battle, he was going to live alone, he was free - he was free!

Right.

* * *

In the summer of 2001, enough money had been put together to afford a trip to Pakistan. The first since they had left the country. Again, the same discussion: who should go?

- "Khalima was just a kid when she left Pakistan, we should bring her!"
- "Yes, but Ibtihab misses his friends and is begging to go, we should bring him."

Eventually they had come to an agreement: Sameer had been away from Pakistan the longest; he was starting to forget about his land and the true values in life… he should go! Again, Sameer didn't oppose. He was happy to see his old friends, happy to see his land and the place he remembered like a playground, a time when he chased chicken and stole sugar canes.

Applauses burst in the restaurant now crowded with the familiar faces of the habitués. Bobby and Jimmy had gotten up on stage and were tuning their guitars. The rest of the gypsies were laughing and smoking in their booth, amusing a couple of pretty eastern European women who had recently joined them. Anor winked at Sameer from across the room. The alcohol was flowing. He'd get a good tip tonight. Bobby ran his fingers across the chords, shushing the audience, and started granulating a fast flamenco tune, his puffy fingers flying over the strings, moving so fast they disappeared, you could not follow them anymore and the music just turned magical. On the left, sitting on the wall bench, Kristin was clapping her hands, her whole body vibrating, asking for movement, begging to stand up and dance. She must have felt his gaze on her back because she turned and sensually waved at him before returning to her trance, absorbed in that insane music that just kept going faster and faster, erasing everything around it. Sameer felt blessed. He was finally feeling truly happy in this country. Finally he felt like he belonged.

* * *

On July 28, 2001, Sameer had returned to Pakistan for the first time in six years. When they'd arrived in Chargulli, everything had felt weird. The city was small and dusty. Everybody was looking at him. Last time they'd seen him, he was a kid running after anything he could eat and getting aroused on American chick-flicks. He had come back a well-shaved man earning more in a night of bartending that they could ever make in an entire month of slaving. He felt awkward. A stranger among his own. After the compulsory parade of aunts and uncles, neighbors and relatives, Sameer, paid a visit to his old friends, nearly expecting to find them unchanged, taking a bath in the river, or lying around in the dirt, talking about the great things they'd do when they'd be grownups. Qasim would become a respected merchant, earning lots of money from all the beautiful things he would sell to the ladies: nail paint, brushes, high-heeled shoes, and colorful Indian saris for their wedding. Najib would become a world famous bike racer. He'd tour the world on his Honda and win prizes for his sensational acrobatics. Sameer didn't really have a dream. Mostly, he would dream of a quiet and safe life where is father would never have to go fight anybody. In reality, deep inside, he dreamt of falling in love and being like those handsome movie heroes living passionate love stories with splendid women. But he'd never told his friends that… they'd think he was a sissy!

Najib had set the meeting at his place. He still lived in the same house and the whole family was still there. It was crowded, noisy, and dramatically simple, just like back then. There were kids running around and women hiding behind the curtains that separated the living room from the kitchen. In the living room, the mattresses where they slept at night had been folded and pushed against the walls to serve as sofas, just like back then. Qasim arrived, a tiny woman by his side. Her belly was full and a baby was sleeping in her arms, his mouth wide opened and his fists clutched to his mother's blouse. She introduced herself quickly and disappeared into the kitchen, shy and submissive. Sameer thought of the Chargulli women from his childhood, always shouting and laughing. All day long their chip-chip-chip would buzz in the patios and kitchens. Six years later, despite the five women crowding the kitchen, he heard nothing but a gloomy silence and the clicking of the pots.

Najib explained he too had a wife now, pregnant as well. She was staying with an aunt because she was having complication with the pregnancy and needed care.

- "So how's Amriki?"

Since his departure, everything had grown much worse in the area. The Talibans were controlling their every move. The secret movie store had been destroyed and its owner hanged. The old sufi babas who sang those beautiful Qawwalis were all dead. All day they'd work and pray, work and pray. Najib wasn't riding bikes anymore. There was no time for that. Qasim's dad had been killed two years before trying to smuggle goods into Afghanistan. So Qasim had taken over the shop but half of the merchandise had been seized by the Talibans. Beauty articles, books, music, it had all been prohibited. He was left with selling canned food, anorexic chicken, and powdered beverages, at luxury prices considering that obtaining even basic supplies was becoming more complicated and dangerous by the day.

Sameer had looked at his friends. What to say? That he lived in a house with three stores and four bathrooms? That he had seven roommates, men and women, from all origins and of all sexual orientations, who were all busy saving the planet or something of the kind? To each question he would answer vaguely feeling embarrassed, guilty, and ashamed.

- "But how's Amriki?" Qasim insisted.
- "Good, all is good."

Sameer had left his friends feeling sick. He'd wanted to give them money but he didn't want to make them feel humiliated. He'd wanted to tell them to come to the US too but he knew things didn't happen like that. He knew he had become a foreigner in his own country and nothing could reverse that. Of course he did not know, at the time, that in just a couple of months the US would declare war on Afghanistan. How could he have imagined then that by the time he would return to his privileged life, he would have become not just a foreigner, but an enemy?

When he had gotten back to the family house, he had found his parents and uncles sitting in a circle with a bunch of people he didn't recognize.

- "Son, this is Mister Mohmand, his wife Gul Ghutai, and their daughter Naghma. Come join us. Sit here my son. Sameer is a very good boy Mohmand-ji. He works very hard every day you know. He is very good with his mum too. Always treats us very well. As you know, he is an American citizen. So we can make the papers for your sweet Naghma."

Sameer went deaf. In his mind, he was replaying the past 17 months. She had fooled him! Shazmina had never consented to him living alone. Of course she never missed an opportunity to remind him of how wrong it was for him to live away from the family, sharing his house with unrelated women, American women on top of it! Yet, she had been surprisingly mild in her opposition.

Despite the music, the smoke, the palmas, and although Kristin was now dancing like a goddess, curbing her perfect body with such ease, Sameer could still see himself perfectly, sitting in the middle of all those people, facing a woman he had never met before, being asked if he had anything against marrying her. What a trick! The mullah had no interest in what he or she wanted. The question was whether they had any good reason to oppose the marriage. "I don't want to" clearly was not a good-enough reason. He tried to think of a better reason but nothing good enough came up. She wasn't ugly, or fat. She didn't seem a bad person, and she belonged to the same people, the same culture. "Our blood is our home". Maybe it would feel nice to have somebody by his side who could understand him, think like him, cook him Chicken Karahi, and teach his future children the Pathan values and traditions. Maybe it would feel like being in Pakistan and USA at the same time. Meanwhile, looking at him, Naghma had done the same equation. He was rather cute and was earning good money over there she had heard. Then she could go to the US. She actually wasn't too excited about that. Her parents had always described the United States as a place of sins and depravation. Americans denied the existence of God and women were treated like objects, she had heard. She thought of it with a mix of disgust and curiosity. Then she'd started thinking about her life in Taliban-controlled Peshawar. It wasn't like she had much to lose. She thought that over there she could go back to study, to travel, and in a few years she could have kids and have them grow away from war, repression, and extremism. No, she couldn't find any good reason to refuse this marriage. So she had remained in silence and nodded when the mullah put her hand onto his.

The frenetic palmas of the band brought Sameer back to the present time. He chased away the images of the twin towers crashing black fumes of smokes and the reporter announcing the beginning of the war against his father's homeland, Qasim's homeland, Najib's homeland… His homeland? He pushed away the thoughts of his wife still obediently waiting in Pakistan for all the documents to be arranged. Instead, he only wanted to think about that beautiful girl dancing in front of him, about the glass of wine in his hand, about the music in his ears. He joined his hand and started clapping trying to keep up with the rhythm one-two-three, one, two; one-two-three, one, two. He was still clumsy but he didn't care. He was here, right now, enjoying life, being free and happy, in love with Washington DC, in love with this land which had become his land. He was Pakistani, he was Amriki, he belonged to the whole world and the whole world belonged to him.

* * *

Around 2:30 a.m. Sameer decided to take the metro to his parents' home. He was a bit tipsy and he wanted to share his happiness with his younger brother who had recently turned eighteen. He wanted to tell him not to get married but to enjoy life and go to university and meet a girl and be happy. Yes, most of all, be happy - that was the most important. Lost in between his thoughts, his joy and his slight inebriation, Sameer was watching his reflection in the window, smirking at himself.

He didn't see them approach. They were three, they were big, but he did not see them coming. As soon as the doors closed onto the Cristal City metro station, they circled him.

- "Hey, Al Qaeda!"

Sameer wasn't listening. A heavy hand fell on his shoulder. He turned over, found himself facing some sort of a bulldog with flaring nostrils and a tattoo of a cross on his bicep with the inscription "God's Will".

- "Watcha thinking about, "Al Qaeda"? Huh? You wanna bomb this city, right? You come here to destroy our country. You Muslim people are all the same, murderers! Now it's time for you to go to hell, motherfucker!"

From behind, an arm grasped his neck, nailing him down to his seat. Half a second later a combo snapped his jaw into his face, within a instant he could taste blood in his mouth. He raised his hands, tried to grab something, some hair maybe. A straight punch stopped his desperate search, reduced his stomach into mashed potatoes, the taste of blood again rushing through his mouth. He could not really feel pain, all he could feel was energy rushing through his body trying to kick, punch, grab. Anything that could free him from that arm crushing his neck. But they were three and they were trained. By the time they reached the next station, a final punch on the temporal lobe knocked him down.

* * *

When he regained consciousness, he saw two blurry faces. He tasted blood and shame. In a state of panic he was waiting for another punch to come and couldn't help but beg God it were his mum bending over him. He closed his eyes and was brought back to his first fight as a child. He saw his *dada* looking straight at him with his right index pointing up straight. "It's okay boy. You're a Pathan, a warrior. A thousand times they will knock you down, and a thousand times you will stand up and walk with your head high. But the day somebody touches your family, your woman, you brothers, then you shall have them taste blood and shame." He felt a hand on his shoulder, then a shake. He opened his eyes in a whim, looking in terror for the face of his aggressor.

-   "Are you alright?" asked a rather disgraceful woman.

Her lips were so big that in his distress Sameer thought she was going to suck his face off.

-   "Hey, dude, you alright?" she repeated sounding quite annoyed with the situation.
-   "I think so", hesitated Sameer.
-   "Alrighty then, I gotta go now. Be more careful, next time."

The other face belonged to a man in his thirties; his expensive suit wore beer spots and smelled like cigarette.

- "Great, I'm gonna go too then. A piece of advice though: don't get yourself noticed too much for a while. You and your people are not much wanted here nowadays."

Right.

Islam is a religion in which God requires you to send your son to die for him. Christianity is a faith where God sent his Son to die for you.

As he walked through the dark to his parent's house, he remembered those words Attorney General John Ashcroft pronounced on the radio after the 9/11 attacks. He barely paid attention to it at the time. "I mean, what did Islam have to do with all of it? These damn attacks are about politics, how can't this guy get that? Sure those men were Muslims, but they did not send their son to die. They killed themselves for what they believed in. Isn't that what US soldiers did in Vietnam and those stupid wars they've been in? Maybe it was the Government, not God, to ask citizens to send their sons to die in its name. Where's the difference?"

Now Sameer was feeling angry and frustrated. He hated those guys who put dirt on the name of Islam. They were so stupid. "What did they try to do with this damn plot, huh? Because of them people died, Americans got a reason to occupy Afghanistan and plough its resources, and hundreds of people in the US are being attacked just for "looking Arab". Stupid Americans. They didn't even know the difference between an Arab and an Afghan. They did not even now where Afghanistan was. Bin Laden wasn't even Afghani. He was nothing. Nothing!" Sameer punched angrily into a wall, hurting his knuckles, something clicked inside his ribcage. He was so full of rage he could not care less about pain. He just kept walking. He wanted nothing more but to be with his family right now. He had to warn them. His sisters would have to stop wearing the veil till things would calm down. Insh'allah they would. Insh'allah.

Shazmina opened the door. The moment she saw him she knew this was nothing like all those times he came home hurt from running around with Qasim and Najib. She had been following the news, listening to the radio non-stop for the past six months. Since September, over 3000 attacks had been conducted against Arab-looking people. Most were Muslims, but there were also Hindus, Sikh, or even Christians. With her savings, she bought her daughters second-hand cell-phones so she could keep in touch with them. She wasn't concerned about Sameer though. He was one of them by now, she thought. A *damn American*. The moment she saw him, her whole body shivered with pain and hate.

- "Ma bache! MA BACHEEEE!"

She started crying compulsively. This wasn't right. They had done nothing! Hamid called the police, reported what happened.

- "I'm sorry sir, there's nothing we can do."
- "What do you mean there's nothing you can do? My son was attacked in the metro, there were witnesses; you can conduct an investigation."

- "Look, sure, I've better things to do – alright? Your son is alive, now keep an eye on him alright. You never know kids today. Are you sure he didn't provoke these guys?"

Silence.

- "Right. Ok. Thanks anyway, Sir… Have a good night."

Hamid put down the phone. He felt humiliated, sad, angry – all at once; but there was nothing to do. He had been an Army Major in Pakistan. Yet, he had accepted any job since he had arrived in the US. He'd cleaned toilets and collected garbage if needed; he never protested, never complained. Anything for his family, that was his Pathan pride. Now what? What was he if could not even protect his children?

He went to the living room where Shazmina was cleansing her boy's wounds.

- "It'll be alright, son. It'll be alright."

* * *

After the events, Sameer decided he needed to be with his family. He left his house on U Street, the red roof, the brick wall, the giant king-size bed. He left the Coppi family, the neighborhood's beer pub with its crazy owner, the corner shop with the big-smile girl. He left the jazz and the flamenco. He went back to the Qawwali and the home-made chicken karahi. For the first time he understood his father's words, "our blood is our home", a sentence pronounced many years earlier, when the words *home* and *homeland* still meant something. "You can never break a Pathan", had said his father back then. Now Sameer was watching his father leave for work at dawn and return only long after the sunset, bent under the weight of unrealized dreams and crushed hopes. An entire life dedicated to provide his family a safe place where to rest, like his ancestors in the mountains of Mehter Lam. Two continents and an ocean he had crossed to get his family to safety. All for nothing. He did not cry. He did not beg. But Sameer could see, behind the roughness of the skin, behind the pride of the eyes, his father's spirit had been shattered into pieces.

Our blood is our home. And so Sameer went back to being a Pathan; a Pathan who defends his family from danger and humiliation. But what could he do? He had no gun, no big muscles, no power. He had left his job and his freedom at *Coppi's* and found himself a prisoner contemplating his uselessness.

"Knowledge is power!"

It was around the time Sameer had announced he was going to America. Qasim had been a bit jealous of his friend's luck. He would do his best not to let it show, but it did show anyway. So a couple days later he came back with his own announcement:

- "I'm going to take evening classes in Peshawar!"
- "You, study? Who's ever seen a donkey go to school?"

Sameer and Najib loved to remind Qasim that he was the wittiest, yet the dumbest of the three. If he had a gift to sell anything to anyone, he could barely add 2 and 2. But Qasim did it. He would ride to Peshawar three times a week to study English and accounting. One day he'd turn his father's shop into a supermarket, he'd say. "Chargulli's first syoopah-markit!" He held onto his dream for years. Till the Talibans destroyed the shop and killed his father.

Partly to honor his friend, partly because he could not picture himself be a waiter his whole life, Sameer decided he would go to university. That was something he could do, at last.

- "I want to understand what's going on in the world, why is my country being torn by wars, why are people throwing planes into the Pentagon. I want to know what's coming so I can protect my family."

The officer at the Bureau of Inscription looked at him with kindness.

- "How about International Affairs, sweetheart?"

She must have been from Ohio. Everybody he had ever met from Ohio was nice and smiling, the women called him "sweetheart" and the men would give him a tap on the shoulder. Maybe in Ohio people had never heard of 9/11. Maybe there everything was normal, still.

- "That sounds about right…"

He wasn't sure what it implied, but he liked the name.

- "Here you go, sweetheart."

The chubby woman offered him a bunch of papers with everything he needed to know about student life, classes, extracurricular activities… there was even a map of the campus. It felt good not to be treated like he could pull out a bomb from his pocket at any time, for once. She wasn't even staring at his Afghan nose like everybody else lately. She was really nice.

Sameer went home smiling at life for the first time since he had been attacked. Maybe things would get better soon, after all. Because of the events Naghma's documentation process had been further delayed. It wasn't safe for her to come. They probably wouldn't let her in anyway. His going to school wasn't helping either. So he had six months left till university, a few more years without being "really" married, and still some time left to believe that things would turn out just fine. "I'm gonna get smart, and I'm gonna get rich."

That was the plan.

5- PYRAMIDS, DONKEYS AND MANDOLINAS

Ramallah, Occupied Palestinian Territories, 2002

The smoke was rising in columns of shame. Tear gas everywhere. Nicola was pressing his *kefia* against his nose, blinking repeatedly to keep his eyes from burning. He retrenched to the hill where shouts and prayers echoed against the blinded occupant. Suddenly an explosion resonated not too far away. Jerusalem, maybe? Everybody froze wondering which side had been hurt. A young boy took advantage of the moment to throw a small stone, which reached its target right in between the eyes. The soldier must have been eighteen years old. Nineteen at most. His skin was dark. He could easily have been a Palestinian. If you stripped him from his uniform. If you stripped him from his armor, the M16, the big boots… if you reduced him to a mere body with used jeans for unique attire, yes he could have been Palestinian. He shouted something in Hebrew. No. Not a Palestinian. A Mezrahi, maybe? Another explosion shook Nicola out of his sturdiness. Bombs and bombs everywhere. The tears in his eyes, the fear in his guts, the anger in his heart. "STOP!" he wanted to shout. "STOP!" he wanted to command. "Why won't they shut up, all of them? My land and my house, my right and my will, my gun against your stones, my rage against your humiliation. Won't they stop demanding, ordering, coercing? No paper, no land: no proof, no right. Won't they stop imposing? And you, with your crazy determination, with your stupid abnegation, won't you stop letting your sons die?"

The soldiers were pushing across the Qulandia checkpoint, forcing him back to Ramallah. A half-faced man came running his way. The blood was invading his clothes, his muscles, his mouth. Nicola tasted the blood pouring in his own mouth. Rage, rage, rage pouring into his body. "VAFFANCULO!" he shouted. "FIGLI DI PUTTANA!" he shouted louder. The image of Yael disappeared, his damn mitigated neutrality disappeared. Tanks were now crushing young bones, tanks were crushing hopes and years of silence. He looked around. A weapon, his kingdom for a weapon! Flattening himself down, he threw a stone right into the Mezrahi's crouch. Under the pain he dropped a teargas grenade. Nicola threw it into the melee. Taking advantage of the confusion, he grabbed the Mezrahi's M16 and shot straight ahead. The gun took control of his inexperience and expelled a few bursts before it crashed into the dust. The gases made Nicola blind. He walked backward, in shock. Cold in his veins. "Did I hit somebody? Is somebody hurt? Is somebody dead? Good for him, then! No, no, no! Me, a killer?" Weakness in his knees. "I am going to sit down, just a minute. (Did I just kill? What happened? I need to see! Let me see!)".

Nicola lost consciousness in the middle of the chaos.

* * *

Remember the road.

Cherish every moment of it.

Cherish the achievement.

Stand in the land of enemies and learn to cherish them as human, looking at them in the eyes, not at the passport. Challenging views, opening to the overwhelming equality of us. *Equals in our hopes as much as in our traumas. Oscillating between statuses – persecutor, victim, occupier, foreigner, stranger.*

Then accept to lose it all.

Cherish the void, the absence of definition.

Let go of our identities.

And discover that we, still, remain the naked humanity of ourselves.

On the morning of his 22nd birthday, Nicola woke up screaming, feeling feverish and anxious. The walls were closing down around him, the outside voices came in feeble, as if from afar. He could barely breathe and felt an urgent need for fresh air. He rushed out of his room, white as a bed sheet. The winter wind slapped his face but he was still suffocating. He'd been dreaming about his father again. Night after night, the spiteful grin of Don Mario haunting his dreams. In between the buffaloes and the tomatoes, Nicola felt ridiculous. Six years had passed and he was still unable to move on. Every day he saw images of despair on TV, true despair! Children torn into pieces, men exhaling inhuman gurgles of pain, women crying over hundreds of dead bodies. It was everywhere: Ethiopia, Afghanistan, Palestine. And there he was, endlessly regurgitating his insignificant traumas, anesthetized by a tedious life. The chicken, the garden, the vines. His world was so small. If only he had been ignorant, but no, he had to be smart! His mathematical skills were still flakey, but his English was surprisingly proper, deliciously rounded by the bouncy Neapolitan accent. Every morning he'd come down to the village's cafeteria, stand at the bar, empty in a gulp a steaming cup of espresso, and snap open the newspaper. Page after page, he followed – indifferent – the agonizing dissolution of the planet, reading about the Kafkaesque politicians' fights, the enterprises' tragic bankruptcies, and the species inexorable extinction. That day, though, Nicola woke up to realize there had to be something more to his life, a higher purpose. It suddenly occurred to him that, for most people on this planet, his fears must have seemed laughable and his frustrations childish and pitiful.

A few days later, Nicola crammed his backpack with the living essential and took off. He left his darling Campania for the first time, with nothing more in his pocket than his meager economies and a freshly stamped passport. Besides that, Nicola had nothing. Not a diploma, not a name, not even a plan.

Mamma Maria kissed him goodbye as if he were of her own flesh, pressing him against her gigantic bosom, recommending him to a God she'd never cared for. She placed a tomato-mozzarella sandwich and a few Euros in the palm of his hand and ran inside the house to hide her tears. Angela ran her fingers though Nicola's long and messy hair, thankful that he looked nothing like that always-freshly-shaved-and-neatly-combed father of his. Nicola walked away, looking back many times to carve in his memory the image of Angela waving goodbye, her white apron resting on her red skirt, her black hair curling around her face. Even in that peasant dress, she looked like a movie star. He took the train to Rome with only one regret in mind: that he had not been able to avenge her. But he knew that, where he was going, his own thirst for vengeance would lose all meaning. His frustration would disappear lost in the monstrous collective frustration. He was ready to leave his father behind, let him clap out in the dark waters of Naples' harbor, and forget all about him.

* * *

Nicola landed in Tel-Aviv filled with excitement and without a clue of what his future might be like. He loved the feeling. He loved the thrill. He wasn´t the least worried. The first night, he was about to sleep in the street when a heavy man with curly black hair looked at him, that little thing crouched against the wall like a dog. "You like music?" he asked in a perfect English. "Do I?" thought Nicola, but all he managed was a nod. The giant offered his hand – Nicola really looked tiny next to him! – and showed him to his Vespa parked just across the street. A Vespa! No man with a Vespa could be bad. Nicola was not sure where this philosophy came from but he decided to go with it and jumped on the scooter. From Florentine, the bohemian quarter where he had prepared to spend the night, Nicola got projected into a world of lights. They were speeding across skyscrapers, slowing down when they would ride along the sea line. The Mediterranean. His beloved Mediterranean. Even from that side of the world, it looked just the same: shiny, peaceful, inviting.

They parked in front of an old rusty building. Ugly block of concrete. As Ahava – what a name! A giant named Love! – pushed the heavy black door, a flow of music rushed out, just as heavy and black. Nicola stared at the benevolent giant Love and seriously doubted they had landed in the right place. Yet Ahava was already inviting him inside. The end of a guitar solo pierced Nicola's ears; he was already missing the soft voice of Massimo Ranieri and the tremolos of the mandolinas. Then a caress of the guitar. A deep voice took possession of the room. The drums were growling making circles with their voices. The mass transformed into one single body swirling to the rhythm of that hypnotic bass.

- "Ahava! What is that?"
- "Nine Inch Nails, my friend!"

Nicola opened an eye, then the other. He had danced all night, feverishly taking in the rush of new experiences. The rest of the day went on as unexpectedly as the previous one. Ahava was determined to show him *another* Israel, so he took him to meet with followers of Hare Krishna. They preached a *different* Israel. An androgynous boy with a tattoo of Krishna covering half his skull was explaining:

- "Israel land of the Jews, ok, no problem. Now what I'm saying is that I'm Israeli, no doubt, but nobody is gonna make me a Jew. So what? I should go? You see, religion is about you, not about anybody else. No state in the world should tell you what to believe in. Israel is a nation for all, the one place in the world where discriminations should never exist. The Jews they came here so that they wouldn't be discriminated against anymore, but now they discriminate against me and my brothers."

- "And Palestinians?"

The follower of Krishna evaded the question.

- "That's not my problem. Personally I don't see why we can't live all together. Fighting is wrong. Palestinians, they want to fight, all the time. They don't want peace."

Nicola listened to the boy a while longer, but he soon got tired of his idealism. One Israel where all lived free and equals. The more he denied being a Jew, the more his *jewiness* rushed vividly through his vein, almost piercing his porcelain skin. He had read once that all Jew medically suffer from the Stasi persecution syndrome. The article wasn´t serious of course, but the more he listened, the more he observed, the more asserted the sentenced grew to be. Can you escape being a Jew, wondered Nicola. Can I ever escape being Neapolitan? Can I ever escape being Don Mario's boy, son of the Camorra?

He left to wander the streets and process. He reached the beach where a group of young men and women were drinking beer and enjoying the sun. They waved at him.

- "Hey, you! Where are you from?"
- "Italy."
- "Cool! Come, sit down!"
- "So what are you up to? Vacations?" asked a girl.

She had long curly hair and tiny firm breasts. They popped from her shirt, little terracotta peaches, soft and brown. She was stunning, looking at him with her dark eyes – till she turned to her companion. Her profile got invaded by her nose, some kind of deformed pyramid. "Eww" thought Nicola, imagining the impact of that nose against his, how it would crush it. Or was it soft, despite that stone-like appearance?

- "I'm on my way to Palestine", he answered, trying to forget the nose.
- "Palestine? But there's nothing there! Why the hell would you wanna go there?"

The nose was talking again. He had to resign himself to looking at her. In an effort to hide his obsession, he turned to her. She was looking straight at him. "Damn!" How could her face be so beautiful from the front and so disproportioned from the side?

- "I want to learn about anger and frustration."

She looked at him as if he were a strange bird fallen from his nest. "What is she looking at?" thought Nicola. "And, seriously, that nose! And I'm the strange one?"

- "What's your name?" she insisted.
- "Nicola."
- "Hi Nicola, my name is Yael."
- "Hey, Nicola!" called out a muscular guy - hair cut short, perfectly shaved.
- "Yes?"
- "So you want to go and get killed in Palestine, huh? Don't you know it's dangerous there? Those barbarians they'll catch you and kill you! That's how they are! We come from Europe, we *are* *civilized*. Those guys… all they know is blood."
- "Well, if it's about being European, then they've been colonized by England dozens of years ago. I'm sure they are *civilized* too."
- "No-no. I was there two years ago. They put me at the Hebron checkpoint for two months. Every day I stood there doing my job and I watched those people, always planning some terrorist

attack. Even mothers, you know. They hide bombs under their hijabs!"

- "You are in the army?"

- "Yep!" he answered proudly. "Lieutenant Colonel at your service! I did my three years of compulsory service, then I was so good they offered me to stay as Colonel in the *intelligentsia*. You wouldn't believe everything those jerks are doing to try hurt us! You, you don't know of course! The media they always defend Palestine, like they are the victims. But you don't know what I know: the plots, the rockets. They want to kill us. But we got this land straight and fair! We have treaties saying that this is our land. We are only taking what is ours."

- "C'mon. Ravid!" cut Yael. "You know you're exaggerating! You're gonna scare the poor guy. If he wants to go to Palestine it's cool. Then he can make his own mind. If I could go to Palestine, I'd go. I mean it's easy for us to talk. We are here, sitting on the beach, but we really have no idea what it's like on the other side. I got posted at a checkpoint too, for a while, remember? It was so damn scary! But it's a particular situation. You don't know how they are in their house. Say, I wouldn't look at you nicely either if I were in their position."

- "If you'd go, they'd kill you in no time!" protested Ravid.

- "But I'd die having seen the *other side*!" laughed Yael – using a deep scary voice.

The conversation went on for a while. The Colonel defended Israel with supposedly historical facts and figures, while the others drank and made jokes, completely careless, detached from all these boring matters of war, disinterested in the *other side* – as she called it. Nicola was listening attentively, learning *official* numbers of Jews killed by Palestinian bombs and missiles, discovering the many twisted plans all Muslims were contriving in Ravid's mind.

-      "It's a global plot, even Al Qaeda is behind it, *I'm sure of it!*"

Ravid was funny, like a robot repeating the second act of the Hamlet. Yet Nicola had a hard time concentrating fully on the debate. On his left, the sun was disappearing behind his newfound Cleopatra, watering her with a halo of gold. The more he looked at that pyramid of a nose, the more his initial repugnance transformed into fascination. By the time her face got lost into the darkness, Nicola knew he was in love.

* * *

Nicola opened his eyes. He was sitting on a plastic chair. A valve movement made him gasp, nauseous. "The gun!" He remembered. "Did I…?" He tried to move but realized he was glued to the chair. His arms were held behind him, tight up together. Everything was moving around him. As he tried to turn his head a little to glance to the side, a strident pain crossed his jaw. A punch? Yes, somebody was punching him. Who? Where? A voice yelled at him in Hebrew. He tried to look in the direction of the howl. The voice again, in Arabic this time.

- "English!" he answered – louder than he had wanted.

A silence, then again in Arabic:

- "Ma ismuk?"
- "Ismi Nicola", then he tried in Hebrew: "Ani Italiano!"

Pain. Another punch in his jaw. In the same point exactly. Dammit.

- "Ani Italiano", he tried again. "Ani min Napoli!"

He was mixing Hebrew and Arabic, he knew it. So he said the only Hebrew word he could remember in that very moment – sorry – again and again.

- "Slih'a, slih'a, slih'a!"

A bright light invaded the room. The soldier who had been yelling at him was young, Nicola's age probably.

- "You took the gun?"
- "What happened?" screamed Nicola. "Did I... kill?"

His big blue eyes were interrogating with despair. He wasn't a murderer. He had known he could never be a killer since that gloomy day on the docks, when he had had the occasion to kill his bastard father and had stood immobile, trying to find the strength to avenge his mother; but he had remained still and speechless. Coward. He was not a killer; he was just a damn coward. *Un fottuto scoglionato.*

- "No, you didn't make it. Nobody died. Still you are accused of attempted murder and will be punished accordingly."

The teenage soldier was trying to sound fierce but his voice came out falsetto-ish. He clearly was uneasy about interrogating a European. Nicola wanted to cry but not a tear came out. The soldier slammed the door behind him, leaving Nicola alone with his fear.

"Idiot! You could have stayed in Tel-Aviv! Lie on the beach, get a job in a bar, go out every night. Away from the traumatized world, not 'having to' anymore, not even 'having' at all. Just living. That's the beauty of Tel-Aviv. All those people trying not to care about the conflict, about settlers lapidating Palestinian families, burning their houses, fighting against their own Army, entitled by God Almighty. But settlers are enraged; Tsahal is looking, awaiting orders. The Army doesn't think, it is not an institution governed by a hierarchy of people, it is a blinded giant. Hit the red button, it kills, the blue one, it yells, the green one, it nods... where is the self-destruction button?

We all care too much. I care too much, and for what? I should have taken example on Ahava, and the Hare Khrisnas, and all those youngsters at the beach. I should have learnt from them: Mr. X died, Mrs. Z was attacked - so what? Not my life. Not going to change the world, make it better or worse. You want my house, my land, my place under the burning sun? Whatever! No, we have to fight, we have to demand a better tomorrow! The stones fly. They land in the sand in a *thub*, the dust remains suspended in the air for a few seconds, then back to the ground where it lays, inert. Let's rewind. Centuries of conquests: Gaul, Rome, Arabia, the Ottoman Empire, the Inca Empire, Spain, England… Shame on Israel! Let's hide behind our safe treaties. Settlers are throwing swords, Palestinians are throwing rocks, diplomats are throwing words, and nations are throwing empty peace treaties – whatever! Palestinians have been deprived of their rights, dispossessed of their land, destroyed, defeated, disillusioned. So I was asked to take sides, denounce, support, join the cause! I will not take sides. I will not tell you that Palestinians are right and Israelis are wrong, or vice-versa. I will reject Manichaeism and definitions for there is no good or bad, not in this war no more than in any other. Is there honor in fighting a hopeless battle? Human rights, *un cazzo*! So much hypocrisy. Self-victimization. Pride. On both sides. They have to win, show the world they were right. Mothers: you are sending your children to war. Fuck the Israeli mother! Screw her who cares about living in an all-Jewish land more than keeping her child alive… Fuck the Palestinian mother: her child opposes guns with mere stones and yet she speaks of patriotism and honor. Stop throwing rocks! This world is not fair and will not be. This land of yours was invaded and taken dozens of times by hundreds of people throughout history. Pick your battle: your land or your rights and your children's rights? To fight for what is lost or to embrace the only way out for a potential future? Hamas is calling for a second Intifada! In the name of what? God, the Nation, a mere ideal? And while teenagers rise in revolt, following the frenzy of the big Mukawama, Hamas, tucked under the blankets, hugging the pillow… Hamas dreams of power and vengeance.

To die for ideas, alright. But of slow death… but of very slow death.

Morire per delle idee

L'idea è affascinante

Per poco io morivo

Senza averla mai avuta."

In the silence of his cell, in the absurd of his situation, Nicola took upon whistling. He ran through the entire song, till the last note, trying to escape the silence, that damned silence that made his thoughts echo against the filthy grey walls, boomerang back to him feeding his anger, straight to where it hurt, the memory of who he was: a well-fed Italian kid.

He tried to calm himself. All this rage was useless. He was tight up, in a cell. Nobody knew where he was, nobody was worrying, probably. He could be held in that cell for months, and the only people who would care were far away, plucking tomatoes and rosemary in the fields of peaceful Marzanello. Yael's face appeared in front of him.

"Maybe she would worry, maybe she´d realize I'm gone… Yael. Pure. Courageous. Yael."

* * *

After a year of military service, after she was posted at that checkpoint and looked into the eyes of the "terrorist", Yael deserted. Of course they arrested her, gave her the option: three more years of service and all would be forgotten. Else, the *Kele*. "No!" she had said. "I won't fight" she had told her General of a father. The General had been torn for about five minutes. Five minutes of doubt: that's all that was left after 24 years of lobotomization. Brainwashed and dedicated, the General had sent his daughter to jail. It was the price to pay to refuse serving Israel. Yael never held it against her father. He was a robot and she would have become one too if she had given into the deal, if she had served her country like a good Israeli citizen.

After Ravid had left, after they'd pushed far into the night their desire for each other, drinking from each other's words like Omar Khayyam drank till dawn the wine he so praised, she'd told Nicola that she had never felt as free as during her time in jail. She felt free for going against the norm, for resisting, for refusing the established order. In her words, in the way she moved her hips, in the softness of her hands, he had found Angela. Young and beautiful Angela, ferocious mother who had freed herself from her own oppression. Angela who tore down her own wall; it wasn't Berlin, it wasn't Palestine, but it was her own prison wall. Without even thinking, he had taken Yael in his arms, embraced her as a brother. She was family. Without a hint of surprise, she had let her head weigh against his chest.

"Beautiful rebellious Yael. Where was she now? Protesting

against the war, taking pictures of the battle, or still in Tel-Aviv, partying at the beach?"

That last thought filled his stomach with another gasp of nausea. He shouted:

- "Bathroom! Toilets!"

Nothing.

- "Sherooteem, bevakasha!"

A young girl opened the door. She seemed annoyed. Her nails were half painted. Clearly Nicola had disturbed her in her effort to feel beautiful, despite the uselessness of it in such a place. She appeared rather ridiculous in her army suit, sweating under her helmet and holding her gun as if an expensive bag. She really had nothing to do here. She hated it and made it quite obvious. Despite the attire, she looked quite feline (a young Gigliola Cinquetti stripped of her prudery) – a sassy seductiveness only accentuated by the leery expression on her face. She took off his handcuffs, holding Nicola at gunpoint. He stood up, a bit dizzy, and his tender eyes crossed her supercilious frown. She startled, finding him perilously yummy. She was missing the sparkle, the party life, the hours making out with some handsome boy behind her parents' back. She pushed him down the hall, watching the muscles of his back move under his dirty shirt.

The "toilets" consisted of a hole in the floor where hundreds of prisoners like him had left their mark. It didn't help. Nicola's stomach was protesting heavily. The girl was ogling him like a cat sniffing at an anchovy. For a moment Nicola thought he had read desire in her eyes, but he chased away the thought. Ridiculous! He resolved himself to pee, shushing the need to vomit. Back to his cell, handcuffed again.

- "Toda" hazarded Nicola.
- "Al lo davar". You're welcome.

Yet she wouldn't leave. She stood there – a fish out of its pound –, her mouth open as if she were to say more. He locked his Neapolitan-blue eyes in hers, taking possession of her, cruelly kindling her desire. Finally, she walked to him, grabbed his hands and undid the handcuffs.

- "Put on if come!"

Her English was catastrophic. Softly, Nicola stood up. Slowly, with a newly revealed self-assurance, just as if he had been born to seduce and manipulate, he raised a hand to her chin.

- "Tu si bella" he murmured in his dialect.

Big blue eyes: that was all she could see. She felt a pulse down there, a fantastic palpitation of her sex. Something she hadn't felt in two years. Something she thought had died inside her that first time she saw a woman being raped. What some of her "colleagues" were doing there… it made her sick. She had not found the strength to pleasure herself since. Yet, inside her big black boots, her feet lifted themselves up on their toe. He leaned in, still burning her with his devilish blue eyes, and she felt the pulsation deep inside her grow stronger. Aggressively, she stole his lips, licked the salt off his lips, bit the fear off his lips, sucked the anger off his lips. Then she shook, panicked, stepped backward, swiftly left the room, locking the door behind her, leaving him alone in the dark, stupidly and uselessly erected.

Nicola spent four days and three nights in that cell. He never saw anybody again. Only an unruffled soldier who would give him a few drops of water and a piece of bread a couple times a day, without uttering a word. The girl had disappeared. They never came back to interrogate him either.

On the morning of the fourth day the muted soldier finally led him down the hall to the excrement-filled hole. As the soldier turned around to let him defecate, Nicola took off his handcuff still left open, threw them over the soldier's head and blocked them around his neck, pulling towards him to strangle the guard. He heard the gurgles of the man, trying to shout to alert the others, but Nicola kept pressing his glottis, cutting the air, impeding the sounds. It's only when the body started giving up, when the man's efforts to free himself softened dramatically, that he realized what he was doing. Shaken, he threw the handcuffs away, let the half-dead man collapse against the floor covered in pee and feces, and precipitated along the corridor towards the exit door.

The handle easily gave up, revealing the outside world bathed in a blinding golden light. Nicola expected to be shot in the back, trailed by the soldiers, hit by a thousand bullets. Nothing came. He trotted into the desert for as long as his weakened legs could carry him. Where was he? Where to go? He had no idea. A movement of his bowels indicated him the way: the nearest bush. After four days of drastic diet, his stomach was devouring him from the inside. He relieved himself in the middle of nowhere, nearly crying out of relief.

As soon as he pulled his torn trousers back up, though, he acquired consciousness of his situation. No shade, a burning sun, no indication, no life. The adrenaline kicked in, providing him with the energy to walk despite his pitiful condition. He chose to go against the sun – assuming he was somewhere west of Palestine.

A few hours later (he must have walked a good twenty kilometers), a donkey came his way. In his delirious state, Nicola received it as a sign of salvation sent to him by the Almighty himself. "Lead me to civilization, O donkey angel!" The donkey led him to Nahaleen, Km17 on the Hebron Road. South of Betlehem. He looked around. He was surrounded by settlements. Great… now what? The donkey was trotting up a tormented road. There was nothing to do but follow it. The path was bordered with burnt, scrawny olive trees; the ground, gurgles of dirty crimson vegetation. No sign of life. "Stupid donkey where are you leading me?" muttered the escapee. As if he had understood him, the donkey stopped and took to inspect the desolated ground for something – anything! – eatable. "Damn donkey…" Sick, frustrated, exhausted, Nicola reached the top of the hill. "A house? A Palestinian house!" A woman trapped in a white hijab opened the door just in time to see him lose consciousness and fall among the rocks.

Surrounded with Daoud and Dahlia's care, Nicola started recovering fast. They were a warm couple, generous and highly educated, with a stunning positive outlook on life. The burnt olive trees surrounding his house, the rusty pipe that channeled the water away from his farm and straight up to the settlers' hills, the waif-like donkey with whom Nicola held long un-responded monologues about his fears and doubts… none of that seemed to affect Daoud and Dahlia's merry disposition. Strong in their conviction to be right, they would let it all glide; only responding to the constant attacks with a warm smile that would reveal the chaos of their teeth.

Every morning, Daoud would go down to Nahaleen to bring home sesame bread, which they'd eat with hummus and *zattar*. Nicola would help Dahlia mix the herbs for the *zattar* (a spoon of oregano, two of thyme, sesame, salt, a few fennel seeds upon Nicola's request, and a generous gulp of local olive oil). Sitting in the kitchen, Nicola would watch her rugged hands knead the herbs, day after day discovering Daoud and Dahlia's story of strength and patience.

- "For 17 years, we have been pleading our case before the Military Court and the Supreme Court. For 17 years, my husband's only aim in life has been to stay on this piece of land, facing the settlers' harassment, spending incredible amounts of money on lawyer and administrative fees. Palestine", she explained in her perfect English, "used to be a land of farmers and Bedouins who could not care less about papers, titles and names. Our country had no names and no borders that we knew of. We lived simply with a few sheep and a donkey on a piece of land that we had acquired through a handshake. When the Jews came, mostly from Eastern Europe, they brought with them a tradition of writings, contracts, and official declarations. They would come to the farmers and declare to own that land by the Will of God. *No, this land is mine*, would say the farmer. *Prove it*, would say the Jew. Since the farmer had no proof and the Jew had a gun, history was made and the conquest continued."

But Daoud had papers.

- "Papers?" – Dahlia laughed – "Rather parchments delivered by Jordan, and by the Crown of England, and by Ottomans! Centuries of papers declaring this land as pertaining to our family: the Nassar family. But the Military Court ruled: "Proofs are not sufficient". Ah! So we took the case to the Supreme Court. They keep asking us for more papers and more proofs so, to this day, the sentence keeps being delayed.

She paused for a while, although she did not seem sad or angry. Just calm. She just sat there in her white hijab and looked at her hands resting on her laps. Then she considered Nicola, with a slight condescending smile on her face.

- "Not long ago, the settlers offered us a blank check. Any price, a lifetime of luxury anywhere we want in this world. But Daoud said no: *This land is my mother and my mother is not to sell.*"

She sighed and fell silent. Maybe she was thinking of what her life would be if they would just let go. Maybe she was wondering if it was worth it... She stood up, determined:

- "We are not giving up, ever! You European boy, you can't understand. You don't know what it means to watch your enemy win. You think it's just a piece of land. Yet look around you, look at all those perfectly blinding white houses. They have pink and purple flowers everywhere. It's so pretty. You think you can go there and ask for help? You think they'll feed you hummus. *Sifr*. Nothing. They won't even let you in. They have built barriers all around their shiny houses. You see those towers? Those are water towers. They steal the water from deep in the ground, growing deserts around their little paradise. They cheat, they steal, they kill, yet we are the terrorists, yet we should let go?"

Nicola felt ashamed. She was right: he had no idea. There was no way he could understand. He could only nod and listen.

"How do you live through nearly sixty years of conflict?" he wondered. "How do you not give up? How do you not run away when every hope of yours is met with humiliation? How do you not – indeed – take to the streets and choose the only path that is offered to you: fight a second Intifada? The big traumas of our lives all become so tiny compared to the thousands gigantic wounds of all people around us. We deal with these traumas in different ways, or sometimes we just don't deal with them at all, but in the end, we still bear the weight of what we care about. Too much concern for our future and past, our possessions, friends, families, lands... An egoistic attachment that brings suffering, disappointment, fear and hate. What would happen if Palestinians just stopped caring, if Israelis just grew indifferent, if I gave up trying so hard to make this little life of mine meaningful?"

The image of his father infiltrated Nicola´s thoughts. Like Dahlia against the invader, he had held a tireless bastion against his father. He had fought against a ghost for many years. He knew the name, he knew the place, but it took him so long to gather the courage to abandon his mother, Maria, and Marzanello. After that night he had overheard Angela, he had secretly bought a knife. It took him an entire year to gather enough money to buy it (Maria was only giving him a few hundred Lira a time). He kept it hidden in the garden, locked in a tin box to protect it from humidity. It was quite big, some sort of dagger actually. One day – he had just turned eighteen– he had gone down to the Piazza with Angela. He wanted to buy her a gelato. At a table, a man – rather handsome – had given his mother a long look, hoping to get her to pay attention. But Angela turned to him a closed face: that of a woman who had given up on love. For the very first time, Nicola dimensioned his mother's loneliness and everything she had given up in exchange for their freedom. The realization that Angela would forever deny herself the bliss of love moved him and enraged him.

The very next day he was hitchhiking to Napoli, determined to plant his dagger into Don Mario's throat.

V-E-N-D-E-T-T-A.

Angela had never talked to him about his father. Thus, he had somehow forgotten he was dealing with a man of power. When he reached the Quartieri Spagnoli, the memories came back rushing. *Don Mario's boy*. He remembered the favors, and his dad claiming him as the heir of his helm. He shivered, unsure who to ask or where to go. He stopped in front of Beppe's pizzeria. The heavy greasy pizzaiolo had been replaced with a skinny shiny lover-boy. He ordered a Margherita. When the last bite had disappeared down his throat he asked:

- "I'm looking for Don Mario".

The waiter leaned down.

- "Are you wishing to die, young man?"

Another shiver.

- "No. I wish to give him his due, that's all."

Mr. Travolta rubbed his hands against his greasy apron and raised his left eyebrow, judging his underage client's determination.

- "Va boh, you'll find him at the docks."

The docks? Nicola repressed that one shiver. He threw his napkin into the empty plate, placed a few banknotes in the waiter's hand and took off to the docks, his right hand safely guarding the knife hidden in his shirt. As he walked to the docks, surprised by the vaguely familiar feeling that the city left upon him, bribes of his past started flickering on his retina. Smells and sounds were as thousands of little Proust's m*adeleines* – as Miss Marialisa would say. The docks were livid grey, lost in fumes of petroleum. "Disgusting! No surprise my father hangs out in such place. Fits him well. *Mo' mi uccidono sicuro!"* He felt his rage turn into fear. "You ain't gonna be a damn coward, Nico! Time to be a man!" But the occasion never came. As soon as entered the neon-lit shed, he found himself surrounded by half a dozen guards, a cigarette pinched between their lips, right hand tactically placed over the right side of their belt, uncovering shiny revolvers with metallic grips.

-    "Marioooooo!" shouted Nicola.

One of the bodyguards, the bold one, slapped Nicola across the face.

-    "Don Mario, se dice."

Nicola spat at the pit-bull-looking man. Don Mario's arrival saved him from another cross-face slap.

As soon as Don Mario stood in front of him, straight as an "i" in his wrinkle-less black Armani suit, Nicola realized he still was just a small boy in front of his father. Tall, handsome, his left eyebrow arched in a perfect circumflex, Mario looked a mafia stereotype: a glamorous, elegant, petty, glossy gestured, pigeon-chested ruffian. Nicola had seen The Godfather a couple years earlier – unbeknown to his mother who had made it a point to keep him as ignorant as possible of his mafia past. Stuck in between a replica of Marlon Brando and the hedge of a platform giving way to sadly uninviting waters, the afternoon heat eerily revealing the majestic Vesuvius in the background, Nicola could not prevent an amused smirk to split his face. A smirk just as soon erased by the fear Don Mario wouldn't be as amused and could slap his face off for such an offense – but nothing came. Don Mario was standing, unshaken, forcing upon Nicola a chilling cold gaze.

What was he hoping for, really? That his father would beg for mercy, would ask forgiveness, would explain how he regretted it and had never stopped loving him all along? Instead: his empty pity.

"Let him go" – he had croaked, waving away, just as Israeli soldiers disinterestedly wave at hypnotized drivers of rusty Volkswagens, letting them go through the checkpoint in an act of graceful goodness. Don Mario's boy deserved Don Mario's mercy – apparently. It was the worst that could have happened. Nicola was expecting sadness, regret at least, but all he found was indifference. Tucked in his wrinkle-less black Armani suit,

- "Your mum", he spat, "she took you away from me. I was going to make you a powerful man. Look what she´s done with you instead: a cricket! My son looks like a cricket. That´s fine, I´ll shape you up."

- "Disgraziato e' mierda! You don´t say a word more about my mum!"

Don Mario grinned.

- "A rebellious soul! I'm glad to see my son has not fallen so far from the tree after all! You think I'm your enemy, but you're just like me."

Nicola resisted throwing himself at Don Mario´s throat. He was still surrounded by a whole bunch of bad boys with big guns.

- "Guallaruso! I'm not like you. I'll never be like you!"
- "E nun alluccare! Nun song micà sordo. Calm down, figlio. You don't have to understand it now. But one day you'll come crawling, urging to be with your own. The Camorra is like a wolf pack, son. You may think you´re leaving, but it´s in your veins. You play all civilized till one day you´ll feel your animal instinct invade your guts and that day you´ll come home to us. You're the son of the Camorra, kid. You're Don Mario's boy. You were born that way, and will die that way."
- "Don Mario's boy, my ass!" reiterated Nicola, eight years after his first sentencing.

Daoud entered the room, offering to his protégé a smile mixed with sadness. He had grown fond of that little scallywag and his touching blue eyes. "Here you go!" He handed over to Nicola a crinkled bus ticket. "You use it whenever you want – Insh'allah! Yanee, you are welcome to stay here as long as you need to, of course!"

- "What will you do now?" asked Dahlia.

- "Fight. What else?"

- "Why, son? Why do you want to fight somebody else's war? Go back to Italy, go to university, get a career" supplicated Daoud.

- "I can't. I'm in this too now. You know, in that cell I discovered a side of me that scares me and fascinates me at the same time. Something dark that I need to deal with or it will lead me right back to where I've sworn never to return. I'll fight without weapons, without stones, just like you do. With your land, your papers, your patience… you're fighting the entire Israeli system, destabilizing it. That's exactly what I'll do, in my own way."

Dahlia joined her hand and looked at him with humid eyes revealing pride and emotion. Nicola hugged his saviors for a long time, then he grabbed the rumpled ticket Daoud had left on the table. He was ready to go back to Ramallah. Back to fighting.

Nicola walked down the stranded hill. The donkey followed a few steps behind, watching over him all the way to the road where Nicola grabbed a collective cab. Nicola waved goodbye at the donkey and sat next to a corpulent woman and her sleeping son. He spent the hour and a half trip watching the landscape unravel, stones after stones in a declination of dirty yellows, and century-old olive trees. On both sides of the road, plastic bags, banana peels, and all sorts of trash were repeatedly asserting that the emergency was somewhere else. No sewage system is the least of their problem. Nicola felt in Naples again. He felt a growing tenderness for this torn territory, and a growing passion for its people. As they passed a check point after the other, a spellbound Nicola searched in every posted soldier the unforgettable pyramidal nose of mesmerizing Yael.

* * *

Back in Ramallah Nicola went straight to Ziryab. A restaurant that had become his go-to place since the day he had settled in the city. Tayseer, the owner, was discussing whether to put a new dish on the menu. His hand caressed repeatedly his shiny bold skull. Back and forth. He smiled when he saw Nicola. "Where had you been, beenee? We were afraid the Jews had gotten you. Some even said you had shot one dead! A true hero!" Sipping his whisky-drenched tea, Nicola related the whole story: the jail, the girl, Daoud and Dahlia. Tayseer put a friendly hand on his shoulder and shook his head a little bit. He was Palestinian: he had heard stories of the kind by thousands. Most male Palestinians had spent some time in Israeli jails. Generally being a young Muslim man was enough of a crime to earn you a couple months in the hole. The girls' story did spike his attention though. He wished his time in jail had been as exciting! "Jamila?" – "Eh. Not bad." *She was no Yael* – he protested silently.

The next day Nicola woke up with the first prayer being yelled in his ears, happy – for the first time - to hear the ritualistic caterwauling. Every morning, around 5am, the Mezzuin would start his litany, orchestrating a cacophony in sol major of argumentative roosters. It seemed as if they were arguing with the Uzuns. The Sura of the Cow generally duplicated their rhetorical fervor. From his room hovering over the caterwauling, there was no chance Nicola could lose a single bribe of it. He generally wanted to tear the roosters' throats, transforming them into a delicious hotpot, or a succulent *coq-au-vin*.

"Recipe for the Coq-au-vin" – he would recite vigorously, hoping the rooster would feel the threat and shut it once for all.

"Start by blanching the bacon to remove some of its saltiness. Cook the bacon in water on simmer for 5 minutes, drain. Dry the bacon and cut it into pieces of the size that pleases you better. In a dish place the bacon and brown in the oven for about ten minutes. You will obtain a thick layer of sizzling fat, which will serve as juice. Place the onions and the rooster, ruthlessly torn into pieces. A thigh, a breast, maybe even the neck, if you like it. Leave the rooster to brown in the oven. When the skin starts showing some attractive colors, add garlic, salt and pepper, stock, wine, and herbs from Provence. The bacon may want to join the roasting party at that point. It is time to let him in. Cover and cook until the rooster is tender and the skin crunchy. Remove the bay leaves, herb sprigs, garlic; add mushrooms. Pump up the heat to reduce the juice to a thick sauce. Lower the heat, stir in the butter. Return the rooster and onions to the pan to reheat and coat with sauce. Garnish with parsley and enjoy!"

The roosters never seemed to bother the threat, though.

That morning Nicola did not threaten the chicken, he did not swear at the skies, instead he jumped on his feet and looked through the window at the first rays of sun plunging Ramallah in a bath of gold. He could not see the Wall from there, but he knew it was there, he knew the Wall was standing there and that at his doors young boys and girls were waking up, hating the new day, another one, still, being strong and courageous, another eight hours standing in the dust, bearing the weight of their armor, another day stolen from their youth, another day defending themselves against kids with stones. Another day being a persecuted Jew at war rather than a youthfully careless Israeli at the beach. At the doors, packed in the check-point cages like sheep, young Palestinian boys, tired Palestinian mothers, depressed Palestinian men. Packed in iron cages, 60 years of suffering, 60 years of diplomacy and treaties, 60 years for nothing.

That morning Nicola woke up and knew this would never be his war. Yet, he would fight it. He would throw himself in the battle and show the world that he was no sheep, no coward. He would never be Don Mario´s boy. He would never be a Palestinian. He would be a free man, that man he had not been in the docks, that man he had not been in the prison cell. He grabbed a black marker and, resolved to kill any trace of the scared little kid craving for vengeance, wrote on his unpainted grey wall, in tall letters:

R-E-V-O-L-U-T-I-O-N.

6- WHAT MAY OR MAY NOT BE AT THE BOTTOM OF THE OCEAN

Santiago, Chile, 2002

- ""Ta lista la carne!"
- "Ya poh, pa' ca!"

Juan reached over the impatient hands to grab a piece of juicy meet warm from the grill. He licked all five of his fingers and his wrist where some of the juice had dripped.

- "He! He! He! He!"

A girl reached for him, grabbed his sticky hand and forced him into following the ecstatic movement of the crowd. They jumped together up and down shouting louder and louder "He! He! He! He!" with every jump.

Cristobal passed by:

-   "Where's your beer, Jote?"
-   "Huh? I don't know? *Hueón*, where's my beer? They took it!"
-   "Sure! You just drank it all already, you drunk!"
-   "*Hueón*! I'm thirsty!"
-   "Here, take mine!"

Cristobal placed his can of Escudo into Juan's shaking hand and left with a big smile, disappearing among the shouts and the laughs. She was coming closer to him, laughing with her mouth wide open, revealing little white teeth all arranged straight in line like tiny saints in their white robes. Juan tottered over and slumbered

-   "I like your teeth."
-   "What?" she yelled over the music.
-   "I like your teeth!" and he fell a bit over, his cheek nearly touching hers. "They're like Saints."

She stared at him a bit dumbly, as if she were trying to figure out the meaning of it all. Juan made a tentative to jump but he couldn't control his feet anymore. He stumbled over and found himself nose to nose with her. Unexpectedly, she abandoned herself to that impromptu kiss and took a step forward to glue her lips to his.

Juan was trying to raise his head but he soon gave up. The effort was herculean. He took a moment to recollect his thoughts and figure out his position. The ceiling above was covered in pictures of Che Guevara. "Where the hell am I?" He felt something moving next to him and slowly turned a head of steel to the right. She was there, naked, some jet-black hair stuck to her face. Her lips were slightly opened, and slightly red from the apple *chicha*. Juan remembered, she had said something about *chicha*. How she liked its sweetness. How her grandfather used to make the treasonous liquor every end of summer, in preparation for the Fiestas Patrias. How he'd prohibit her from touching it – not even a shot glass! – before September 17. How he died on September 17, just a few days before the referendum. How sad it was that he never got to see Pinochet leave, how he was never really gone anyway. She talked a lot! He preferred to look at her the way she was now: silently naked.

He poked her with a finger to wake her up but she started snoring lightly instead. Juan suddenly realized he couldn't feel his right arm. Her head was crushing it, preventing him from moving. He started sliding away with great care, even holding his breath, which only caused her to stop snoring for about two seconds, then start again – now growling more than snoring. Something to the likes of a purr. A voluptuous female tomcat's purr. Realizing an 8.5-strong earthquake wouldn't wake her up, Juan slid away letting her head roll heavily onto the other side. He scooped out of bed, teetering in the semi-obscurity for his flip-flops. He couldn't think clearly. Couldn't even hold himself firm. Yet he needed to leave. No attachment: that was his rule. No cuddling, no breakfast in the morning, no sharing the toothbrush. Before shutting the door behind him he gave a last look at the girl curled up in the dim light of the last days of winter. "At least she's pretty" and he smiled, congratulating himself. He was about to close the door behind him when he noticed the morning was bit chilly. He came back to the bed, nearly stepping over his own feet, and covered the girl with the red bed sheets. He stood a minute, trying to regain balance, then finally leaned forward to clear away the ink-black lock of hair still crossing her face.

Outside, the street was deserted. A few cars were sitting quietly along the sides, holding still despite the steepness of the path. Juan walked down carefully, balancing himself against the walls, wondering how the hell he would find his way home. A black dog with a happy face seemed to hear his distress. He trotted towards him, a smile on his face. He stopped a few dog-steps from Juan and tilted his head to the right, gauging his found. He yapped once, as to encourage him, and took to the streets, bouncing on his pawns like a joyous troubadour, watching back from times to times to make sure his protégé was following. Far below, the Pacific Ocean was losing itself among the clouds, only revealing a few fishing boats and commercial ferries silently fencing the waves.

Juan finally reached the beach, the dog celebrating around him. Dog and boy both breathed in the ionic winds, absorbing the cold and feeling their lungs slowly healing from all the smoke from the previous day – for one – and recovering from all the side-street pee-sniffing – for the other.

- "Tell me dog. Isn't life beautiful?" he yelled at the waves.
- "Wuf!"
- "Good boy!" and he petted the beast right between the eyes, winning for himself a thankful shake of the tail.

Around them a few bodies were laying on the cold sand like stranded whales. One of them was slumped on top of the rocks, unaware that the ocean was already coming to lick his feet. He was still holding a half-full bottle of beer on one hand, and a dirty handkerchief on the other. The dog went to sniff the body. "Dogs are like that" – thought Juan. "They don't care if you're a gentleman or a bum; they take care of you just the same." The dog pushed on a leg with his nose but the body didn´t budge. It just emitted a feeble roar, enough to reassure the dog, which turned away, pleased. After making his morning round, sniffing body after body just like a nurse checks on her patients, the dog came back to Juan, happily gave him a big lick of the tongue, and took position by his side, sitting on his bottom, front legs still straight: relaxed yet alert.

Juan was looking amused at the dog. Life was reminding him – once again – how lucky he was. He was about to graduate with all honors, despite his humble origins, in a country where education was everything but accessible to all. The world was about to be his. Juan felt so satisfied with himself at that very moment that he got up on his feet, pulled down his trousers, and childishly mooned the vast

Pacific Ocean and everything that may or may not have been at his bottom. The dog yapped happily, satisfied with Juan's silliness. Suddenly, something caught his eye. He trotted back to the dock, leaving Juan alone.

Juan pulled his trousers back up, closed the zip, sat back down, and crossed his legs. Unexpectedly, a wave of nostalgia invaded him. He sprawled onto the beach, shucking the sand grains in between his fingers. He became philosophical, returning to the early years, when he had felt so dull and life had seemed so gloomy.

Juan knew that there were many ways he could have never gotten to this pleasantly chilled morning of September 19, drunk and satisfied, full of hope and maybe a bit full of himself too. He had celebrated all night the birthday of Chile, feasting on Chile's meaty belly. The *parrilla* may never be empty for the Fiestas Patrias. Steaks bigger than his leg had roasted all night long on the grills of every patio, every *fonda* and every beach of Chile. The meat juice had dripped on every hand of Chile and all of them – without exception – had licked their wet fingers, burped joyfully, and raised a greasy handkerchief to dance some more to the beat of the cueca – teeky teeky tee! He too had raised his glass to celebrate Chile! He too had cheered to the flag, and danced the dance of the *huasos*: landowners, people-owners.

But the morning was misty. If only it had been windy. Windy enough to blow away his thousand unanswered questions. Instead it was suggestively misty. Juan poked a finger into the mist and waved goodbye to the rusted Slate Gray 1978 Chevrolet C10 that was pulling off, leaving him alone with his dead cricket.

The dog came back. He held in his mouth a rumpled newspaper, which he let fall at Juan's feet. The front page was half covered in dirt, but the title remained intelligible: *Young hooded boys set fire to a McDonald in commemoration of the September 11 1973 military coup.*

Juan started flipping through the pages of the week-old issue of El Mercurio. "Kissinger won't be extradited to Chile after all". "Pinochet's health is keeping steady in his million-dollar mansion of northeast Santiago". "Chile commemorates two September 11". Followed a long article about September 11 in the US, and the twin towers, and the terrorists, and bla bla bla. Juan threw a punch right into the word *terrorist*, leaving a tear in the paper.

- "Fucking bastards even stole our September 11. Fucking gringos stole everything from us."
- "Wuf!"
- "You're right dog, they fucked us up. But we're still alive aren't we. There's still time to get back at them, right dog?"
- "Hhh – hhh – hhh." The dog looked intensely at Juan, his head slightly tilted to the left as if his tongue, carelessly swinging on the side of his mouth, were just a bit too heavy for him.
- "Don't you ever wonder, dog, why things happen? Think if I were born in the States. My life would be so different. I probably would not even be able to find Chile on a map, right? Don't you ever wonder why here, why now? I wish I could bring the ocean waves to life. I wish they'd tell me their story. Who they've seen, who they've carried, how many man down being rocked by their

unstoppable comings and goings. Those man, their fate decided upon by other people, life twisted and ruined by big men in big leather chairs."

- "Warf!"

- "I know dog. What am I complaining about, right? After all, I'm among the lucky ones."

- "Awuuuuuu!"

- "Good boy!"

Juan patted him on the head, grateful to have such an agreeable companion. He went on reading. The paper also revealed the list of the thousands of documents, hidden reports, secret memorandum, and secret meetings that had just been declassified. The CIA, Kissinger, Nixon, they all backed anti-Marxist Pinochet. They, from their leather chair in their wooden mansions, decided the fate of millions of Chilean people. Documents after documents revealed that back in 1972 already "the United States intended to cut military assistance to Chile unless they moved against Allende, and that the U.S. desired, and would actively support, a coup". El Mercurio, which had channeled the CIA's propaganda against Allende since the early 70s, was now turning its coat.

Juan hated politics. He did not want to hear a thing about Allende and Pinochet, didn't want to think any more about the torture, the fear, the resistance. He certainly did not want to see any more picture of the Moneda palace being bombarded on that cold morning of September 1973. He only wanted to think of the future, his glorious future as a renowned surgeon. That's what he was going after. He wanted to cut, dissect, open up bodies like he used to with the courtyard bugs.

But again, Juan couldn't help fantasizing about how his life may have been if even just one thing in the uncontrollable chain of events that had made his path so lonesome, had gone differently. For one, he may not have had to go through his teen years alone if that morning of September 19, 1991, Edwards father, owner of El Mercurio and proud *pinochetista*, had paid the ransom for his son.

Agustin Edwards Eastman was never of the obeying type. Within a few hours of the letter's receipt, he had done pretty much everything the kidnappers had ordered not to. María Luisa, his soft-hearted wife, was still holding the letter in her frail hands, reading it again and again – hoping to find a clue as to who was holding her *baby*.

SEÑOR A. EDWARDS

PRESENTE

Your son was held captive today and in these moments is kept in a safe and inaccessible place. He is well and his integrity (physical and mental) in the future will depend only upon you. The aim of his detention is to negotiate his LIFE.

You must strictly abide to our indications; do NOT communicate this situation to the press, police, friends or parents. Whatever step you shall take in that direction, we will find out, thus excessively slowing down the development and culmination of this enterprise.

We are EXPERIMENTED PROFESSIONALS determined to fulfill our goal.

Do NOT make any move.

Be patient.

We will get in touch again.

We commend ourselves to the LORD, praying that we shall get to satisfying terms on both ends.

Maria Luisa begged her husband once more.

- "It is just money. It's not worth risking our son's life. Honey, I beg you!"
- "Don't be silly! You know very well they won't kill him. This is not even political. They just want money and they won't get it if they kill him. We shall not crouch in front of those communist rats!"

The discussion was over. Maria Luisa knew it. She retired to her room and kneeled down to pray God to return her boy. She was feeling guilty. It was her fault. If she and her husband had not insisted so much for him to come back to Chile, he wouldn't be suffering right now. She could not stop imagining all the horrible things he may have been going through. Maybe they were beating him up with sticks, or breaking his hands – like Pinochet's men with Victor Jara, nearly 18 years earlier – or who knew how much worse they could be doing to her little one.

To her, he was still her *little one* – although, to say the truth, Cristián Edwards was not that "little" anymore. At the age of 33 he was already running the regional publications of El Mercurio. He had recently returned from the United States where he had completed his MBA, found romance, and thought he had finally freed himself from his father's grip. But he was a Edwards. You don't so easily escape your name.

He sure must have missed his perfect life in the land of the free while going crazy in that 2x3 meter square box. The music was playing non-stop, very loud. The light was too bright and would go on at random hours, waking the hostage up, making him lose track of the days, the nights, the outside world. His gatekeepers wouldn't talk to him. Who were they? Were they tall, were they short? All these questions had been answered, decorticated, dissected, during the long trial that had established guilty five men and one woman. Cristián Edwards had described the two men who had guarded him: one had a moustache, the other reading glasses. Both used Argentinian accent to confuse the hostage. One had quite a talent for imitation. The other, not so much. There may have been a third one, C. Edwards recalled during the public trial. *May have*? How do you not know? How do you not remember?

Juan had spent so much time connecting the dots, reading the trial's transcripts, Maria Luisa Edward's interviews, the criminal depositions. He even visited members of the Frente Patriótico Manuel Rodríguez in jail. Anyone who could give him a clue as to what had happened back then. With time, and obsessed determination, Juan had recomposed pieces of the puzzle. The abduction, the plan. In total, he had spent two years of his life trying to understand what had become of his father, but Manuel had disappeared without a trace. According to the final verdict, five men and one tiny women took an active part in the abduction of Cristián Edwards. All six were arrested and jailed, some even sentenced to death. Within a few days, four of the men escaped in a big helicopter, cheating the law, ridiculing democracy. The fifth one refused: he could not leave without his woman. Rather a life in jail than a life without her! Some applauded, some called him a fool. To history, though, they were simply six terrorists.

Except there were seven. History forgets cowards.

A year had passed since Aylwin had installed into power. Despite what they would say, everybody had hoped that somehow something would have changed. Sure the raids had stopped. Nobody had gone missing in nearly a year. Nobody had knocked at their door and pulled them out onto the streets, in whatever conditions they were in (naked, peeing, wet, or drunk), to search their home. The fear was less, the violence was less, but none of those who had gone missing had returned, none of the food on the table had returned, none of the "normal" life had been given back. Manuel had knocked at every door. He was prepared to do any job, really. He had been an engineer once, long ago. "We don't need no communist rat", they had told him the day they fired him from his job at the national electric company. Now the tone was softer, the refusal more diplomatic – but in Manuel's life it made no difference. He was branded. Everywhere the answer was the same: "we don't hire communists. Too complicated." Although he had thrown away his party membership and would not mention his past, ever, the signs of his political associations were still written all over his judicial history, and scars of the resistance were still transfiguring his face. Unanticipatedly, all those years resisting started adding up.

Before the dictatorship, Manuel was a handsome young man with a profession. He had just met Mariana. He was in love and Allende was governing.   Now he didn't care no more about politics. He was an old man with too much past and not enough future. He had lost his pride a while ago. He had left his pride smear the walls of Santiago, together with his blood. It had happened over the days, slowly. He had not realized at first. It took many beatings. Many humiliations. Then they had squeezed the last drop from him, they had beat him to the floor. An officer had raised his big black boot over his skull and squashed it in the mud. He had felt the musty ground invade his nostrils, the taste of dirt and pee slipped into his mouth before he could repress his silent shout. When he had raised his head again, he had seen the big red face of the fascist dog spitting into his right eye. Behind the blockades, 6 month-old Juan was crying, looking at him, his tiny tiny hands clutched onto Marianna's blouse.

Over the years, Juan had had plenty of time to recompose every bit of memory. How it started, how Manuel's despair grew, how it led to his demise.

On the morning of December 14, 1990, as he woke up, Juan found his parents sitting at the kitchen table, discussing nervously yet muttering as not to wake up the household. Juan wanted to listen, to be part of the secret, but Mariana hushed him out.

- "Go and play with your cricket, *cariño*."
- "I'm hungry."
- "We got nothing, hijo" sighed Manuel. "You'll have to wait till lunch, till El Pato arrives."

El Pato. Juan shivered at the hated name, and his stomach growled as if answering with a protest, but Manuel dismissed it, too preoccupied with doodling all over his big white paper sheet like a mean penpusher.

Juan spent all morning playing with his cricket. It would be Christmas in just a few days and the December sun was sizzling. Juan hated the heat. If he had had a say, if he were an adult, he would have escaped to Patagonia, live with the penguins and sheep. But he was just a kid, hiding in the shadow of the trees, bugging his cricket with a blade of grass. He knew he was not getting any present. He was not like those kids with big houses and fancy clothes. He would be lucky if there was food on the table for Christmas Eve. He didn't care. He was too busy trying to figure out what the big secrets were about. He knew something was up. He could feel in his guts that his parents were cooking up something. El Pato's visits were never a good sign. He came once in a while to bring boxes of vegetables, but hidden under the lettuces and carrots: dismantled M16s; and in between the corn and the avocados: live bullets; and inside the cabbages: small grenades that fit even in the palm of his tiny hand. "Not now!" he wanted to yell. "Pinochet's gone, isn't he? We can walk in the streets now, can't we?"

Of course Juan was too young to fully understand politics. Aylwin was President, but he was an underdog. And Chile was free, but his father wasn't. Where was he to find a job now? Who would hire him? Who would feed the hundreds of mothers still waiting for their husbands and their son to come back? And worse still, who would allow them to fight for their rights now that the international community was looking elsewhere, happily satisfied with Chile's new Democratic brand.

Manuel sat with El Pato at the kitchen table. He didn't like him much: he was young and arrogant. But he had taken part to Pinochet's ambush and tentative murder. He was a true companion of arms.

- "We can't go on like this, Manuel. Me, I fought since I was fifteen. What am I supposed to do now? I got no career, don't want to be trapped inside some cubicle. We didn't go through all that shit to end up selling hot dogs, *cachai*?"
- "Right" he answered, lowering his head.

He drew a circle in the dust covering the pavement with the point of his dusty shoes. He felt dust even in his throat. He got up, grabbed a glass, filled it with chilled tap water and downed it at once. Meanwhile El Pato was still reasoning.

- "So I got to think. We need money. Enough money to get back on our feet. Not much. We need just a couple million pesos for us and our guys to start our own business, *cachai*. Manuel, do you really want to leave this life of shadows to drawn yourself into the shadow of some boss? Can we ever do that, after all that's happened?"

- "I don't know; but I don't have no money Pato. All I got left is a couple M16 and a bunch of grenades".

- "*Hueón*! That's good! That's pretty good! Listen, we can get that money. All we need is to take it from somebody who's got too much of it. We could be some sorts of Robin Hood, ya know?"

- "What do you mean, Pato?"

- "I mean there are pigs out there who've got so much money they don't know what to do with it. They don't want to give it to us? Fine, we'll take something that's important for them, the same way they took our lives and freedom."

- "What the heck, Pato? What are you talking about?"

- "You know Manuel. You know very well what I am talking about. Say we take somebody from *their* family and ask for a ransom. Say we take somebody from Edwards' family for example. His dear shit-fed son: away from him, okay... Then you'll see how he suddenly opens up his wallet, the pig!"

Manuel had stared at him for a long time. Trying to detect in his eyes what kind of sickness was torturing him. He hated the idea. He had been too long pushed into the role of victim to suddenly think of himself as the torturer. He could not resolve to such extreme solution. Every cell of his brain resisted it. His guts, nonetheless, his heart and his blood, had no problem punching and hurting and kidnapping, and doing whatever to take a chance at revenge. "Revenge. What a funny concept!" – Manuel tried to reason. For seventeen years he had kept hidden in his house enough armaments to blow up an entire block. He'd never used them. He had trained, and practiced, made hundreds of plans, evasion plans, defensive plans, never before had he been given a chance to cross the field, pass the ball, shoot straight to the net and goal! Why now? Why now that it was all over? Hadn't Pinochet retreat to the back scene? Hadn't democracy been restored, and all the well-fed presidents, fancy kings and cocky prime ministers had they not come to acknowledge it, endorse it, and bless it?

El Pato was observing him quietly. Showing no sign of impatience. The emaciated boy plunged a rusted spoon into the washed up black tea. He raised the cup to his mouth and sipped his tea with his lips shaped into a heart so as not to dip his precious moustache. It was but a thin line of dark hair covering his upper lip. He trimmed it every morning to make it look more "gangster" – he'd say. The guys made fun of it behind his back, calling him Freddy or El Queen. El Pato may have killed them if he knew, but they joked about it all the same.

El Pato was looking at Manuel while Manuel was looking at his shoes, his sad dirty shoes, trying to figure out a way to say no without sounding a coward… a way to say no without feeling a coward.

- "Okay."

Manuel jumped in his chair. He had no idea why he had just said that. "Okay? No! Not okay!" He wanted to say no and now it was too late, he couldn't go back. El Pato was already on his feet, smiling, extending a lean and firm hand to offer a shake, a pact-making shake, irrevocable – the kind that is made among brothers, the only kind of shake that warriors know. It was too late and his blood was already boiling too strong. "Shut up!" said Manuel to his heart. "It's too risky, too dangerous. You've got a family, you've got responsibilities for God's sake!" Unfortunately for Manuel, it was pure excitement, not fear, that was forcing him to stand up now, distending his chest, pulling his right hand out of his right pocket, loosening his fingers and dramatically placing his hand into El Pato's hand, palm to palm, strong and vigorous.

Manuel wanted to taste blood other than his own, get back his lost seventeen years of being a handsome young man. He could not shut it up. He had a family and it was his duty to take care of it like a real man, a strong man. Enough of the shame, enough of the humiliation; time for revenge had come!

- "You made the right choice, Manuel. You'll see, we'll get that money and get us and the brothers a fresh new start."

184

- "What's next then?"

- "The operation starts in ten days. I'll be back here on December 22. That give you time to get your shit together and prepare your people. You won't be able to have contacts with anybody during the whole of the operation.

- "How long would that be?"

- "Six months, maybe seven. We want to get it all over by end of June. After that, you come back here, move somewhere nice with your family, and get yourself a whole new life. Once it's all over you won't have to hold a gun ever again."

- "What if we get caught?"

- "We won't. We'll plan the all thing right and make sure we won't. Once we kidnap *el hijo de puta*, we'll negotiate straight and should get it all set in a matter of days. No traces."

- "Okay."

It took Juan many years to understand the true reality of the transition to democracy. Only recently had he realized that if his father had taken part into many "guerilla" actions, he had never been anything more than a political activist. A chained man at war. Pinochet the Dictator was gone, but Pinochet the octopus was still holding strong to power. Juan understood now that for them – the nobodies – the war had not be won, it had just taken another name. If his dad wanted to help his people, he could not do it as a resistant anymore. The laws had changed. The rules had changed. Manuel knew that whatever he was about to do, he would be considered a terrorist for it. The same values, the same goals, the same fight, yet a very different title: terrorism.

Over the next ten days, Manuel sorted everything to prepare for his absence. He wished they could have started the operation later, after Christmas. The thought of leaving his son alone for Christmas tore him apart. He felt his heart hurt in his chest, bigger than a watermelon, ready to fall apart. He had kept in a tin box a few pesos, just in case. He nipped them on the sly, without Marianna's noticing, and went down to the school. Not the one for the rugged kids like Juan's; the one for the fancy brats. The school was closed for summer holidays, but he ran the doorbell, hopeful. The concierge answered: a proper man, with a proper shirt and proper trousers without stitch-ups. A round-belly too: the pigs were feeding him good stuff.

- "I'm sorry to bother you, Sir, but Christmas is coming and I'm looking for a nice book for my son, you know."
- "Is he a student here?"
- "No, but I was hoping you may have some old one you don't use so much anymore."
- "Our books are for our students. Go to the bookstore."
- "I know, I understand, but I'll pay. I just want to buy a book for my kid and I can't afford books from the library. I can't afford a new book, but I thought maybe you got an old one. It don't matter if it's a bit beaten up.
- "Alright, I'll go check. You wait here."

The concierge came back after a few minutes, carrying a tower of books imprisoned in a stranglehold between the man's double chin and the cradle formed by his hands. All had dog-eared corners and ink stains, but they were good enough. As soon as he browsed through them, Manuel knew which one he'd get his little boy for Christmas: "Anatomy for Children".

Late that night, Juan looked at his father leave in an old banger color of ashes. A rusted Chevrolet they'd fix to make as little noise as possible. Manuel had given him a long hug – which had made Juan even more wary: his father was not of the sentimental kind. Manuel had held tight his son's skinny body, then slowly he had revealed a box wrapped in newspaper he had been hiding behind his back.

-   "I know you like playing with bugs. Maybe you'll be a famous veterinarian one day. Or a doctor, who knows! I don't care; just promise me you'll study. Whatever happens, promise me you'll go to university and get yourself an education."

Juan had nodded like a robot. Why was his dad talking about university? What was going on? He wanted to run after him. He could feel deep inside that something was wrong, that he shouldn´t go, that this night would change his whole life somehow. But he didn´t dare. Manuel looked grave, and Juan didn´t want to appear a sissy in front of everybody. So he rushed inside the house instead – erasing his nascent tears with the back of his hand – and resolved to go and check on his cricket. Yet something stung when he passed by the hidden closet carved in the floor. The door didn´t resist as he pulled it up, so he peeped in quickly before Mariana would come in.

The vault was empty, all the weapons gone. He rushed out the back door before Mariana could see him. He needed to breathe. It suddenly dawned on him that his father was leaving. He was leaving to do the only thing he could think of in order to protect his family, feed them and give them a future. He went after the rich ones, the oblivious ones, looking for money. Juan ran outside, his heart ready to explode in his chest, tears bursting from his eyes.

- "Papa! Papaaaaaa!"

It was too late. The rusty Chevrolet was gone, leaving no trace. Mariana tried to take a hold of him. She was torn to pieces by the sight of her son in despair. She had only agreed to the plan out of hope, but at the condition he wouldn´t contact them until the plan was successfully completed. He could not endanger them. He could not endanger her baby.

Juan escaped his mother´s comforting arms. He needed air and space. Alone under his tree, the cricket immobile in his cage, Juan tore the yellow paper surrounding his unexpected gift. The ink stained his fingers a little. He uncovered a dog-eared book, stained on the sides, with scribbles even on the front pages, but still the best book of all: "Anatomy for children". He loved it but right now he wanted to hate it. He did not want a stupid book. He wanted his dad.

Juan curled up into a shivering ball and cried silently while watching his cricket die slowly inside his glass cage.

On October 14, 1991, Manuel sent a letter to Marianna. It was a weird letter, a mix between a love letter and a suicide note. He commented on his difficulty to assume his choices. He talked about his incapacity to accept his uselessness, his being powerless at protecting her, and Juan. But also he talked about his love for her, about how he loved the pimple that blossomed on her right cheek when she smiled, the way he wished to take her out to a fancy restaurant, treat her like a princess, and how pretty she'd look in that red dress he'd buy for her. "And you'll wear a pink flower in your hair, like the day I met you. And we'll have another baby, to give Juan a little brother or sister. If it's a girl we could call her Paz, for she shall never know war or pain. Paz. Do you like it? Mi querida Marianna, I love you. So much that all these years of hunger and fear have been nothing. They have been wonderful, every day, every minute, because you have been by my side. You are so beautiful and I am so weak. You are so courageous and I am so lost. Mi amada Marianna. I don't know if I can fix things up. I try, every day I try, but I don't know if I can do it. Will you forgive me?"

On October 21, Manuel told El Pato that he needed air. They had been fighting about the way the hostage should be held. El Pato insisted he should be kept numbed and in a state of absentness as to limit the risk of him remembering anything after his liberation. Manuel thought the measures were being too harsh and the space provided too small. Fourty-two days had passed since they'd captured Cristian Edwards. Edwards father was still refusing to pay. The negotiation were going nowhere. They had planned to keep the hostage a few days – a week at worse. Fourty-two days were becoming an eternity, putting everybody on edge. After they had exchanged a few strong words, Manuel lit up a cigarette (the first one since Juan's birth) and stepped outside the house onto the street.

On October 22, worried and angry with Manuel not having returned, El Pato phoned Marianna assuming he had fled back home.

On October 23 and 24, Marianna spent day and night calling friends and interrogating neighbors. "Had anybody seen her husband?"

On October 25, Marianna realized she couldn't call the police. She couldn't be sure Manuel had not put himself in troubles, and – in any case – the police force was the very same that had beaten him up just a couple years earlier. None of the oppressors, torturers, murderers had been arrested. Democracy? A name empty of meaning, a curse condemning him to a right-less fight, and her to silence. The dead? Invisibles. The living? Muted. Marianna spat on the floor, mixing her tears with her rage. Democracy? A politically-correct solution to blindfold and gag the undesired! She let a sob bubble out her throat and fell onto the floor, yelling the name of the only man she'd ever loved.

On October 26, Marianna told eleven-year-old Juan that his father was missing and may never come back. As to where he was, she answered that he could be anywhere, from the bottom of the ocean all the way to high up in the skies.

And just like that, Manuel disappeared without a trace, without a word, leaving behind him nothing more than a dog-eared book and a confusing letter.

That letter, Juan had read it a thousand times, searching for clues, showing it to ex *guerrilleros*, ex partners in crime of his dad, hoping they could read into it. Despite it never revealing anything, it still followed him everywhere ten years later, on that gloomy dawn of mid-September.

Sitting back up, with the dog still resting by his side, he took it out of his pocket to read it once again. "Querida Marianna." Yet he could not read on. He felt sick to his stomach. He knew the letter by heart: it was carved onto the back of his skull like a curse. He clinched his fingers into a fist, crunching the letter by the same occasion. Slowly, methodically, he made it into a ball, making a stamp out of his hands, pushing the paper softly into a well-rounded ball the size of a plum. A shout took shape in his throat, which grew to explode into a roar.

- "Enough, dad! I'm done waiting for you. I don't want you in my life anymore! Enough thinking of you, enough wondering! Go to hell, dad! Go to hell, Manuel!"

The dog – awaken by the invocations – had risen to his full height, ready for action. Juan threw the ball at his feet and yelling with all the strength of his lungs, shot into it, sending it high up towards the skies and then down over to the bottom of the big ocean to rest with the thousand corpses of the thousand *desaparecidos*: thousands of men being searched in vain, each of whom may have left a solitary kid wondering whether his father may or may not come back one day.

The dog loped after the ball, provoking a whirlwind of sand to rise behind him, hiding the tears running down Juan's cheeks. In the background, a beached whale rolled over, hugging its bottle of cheap Pisco like a soul-soothing teddy bear.

2012

7- PAKHEYR, YANEE WELCOME

Washington D.C., USA, 2012

The void is opening up below my feet. My toes are already out, contemplating the big nothingness. My whole body is resisting but I know I'm going to do it. I've got no choice. "C'mon Sameer, Jump!" exhorts the middle-aged man behind me. He slightly scares me with his imposing jaw line and cut-through nose. He looks like an army Commander. His salt-and-pepper hair reveals the experience, the years of combat. I'm actually surprised not to find any scar on his left temple. Mister G.I. Joe behind me loses patience and places the palm of his hand on my right shoulder. He waits a few seconds to give me a last chance to decide for myself, but I'm still frozen, my brain sending over my body thousands of electric discharges begging for survival. A push in my back destabilizes me and I fall head first, flushed down like a puppet into the vast emptiness of the deep blue summer sky. Far below, the Potomac is shining like a Broadway diva. As I keep getting nearer and nearer, I can start discerning the dazzling white yachts swooshing their way through the stars.

I'm turning thirty-two today. Every year since 2001, my friends and I have ever done only one thing on our birthdays. After a gargantuesque family dinner with quantities of potahs, karahis, curries and sweets, we'd drive to Virginia Beach, the three of us and our CDs of Pashto music – just to dip our toes into the cold sand color of cement. We'd stay there all night long, drinking and smoking, waiting for the sun to rise over the Atlantic ocean, dreaming about all the wonderful destinations hidden in its tails, and picturing life "back home", where at that exact moment the sun would be disappearing behind the Landi Kotal mountains separating thousands of Pathan families from Afghanistan, estranged land of our ancestors.

This year though, I broke the spell. This year nothing is the same and nothing will be ever again. So, I decided to take the leap. Today, first time in my life, I took the leap and jumped from a plane, 5000 feet above the ground, with nothing between me and death but a piece of cloth.

I'd always wanted to do something extreme but I never had the guts. I've never been a go-for-it kind of person. I have to think and ponder everything. Most of the time, I just end up contorting myself, bending to my family's goodwill. What happened to the mischievous fearless Pakistani boy I once was, I don't know. Every big decision in my life was taken for me, and all I did was nod. I never rebelled, too young as I was to judge the weight of my indecision. It took me years to understand what I had done. What I had consented to. At the time, I was just happy I would have a woman to please me and cook for me. Naghma has been very good to me; she's given me everything a good Pathan wife is trained to give. Unfortunately for her, I haven't been in line with my role.

Monday through Friday, I finish work at 6pm sharp, and before I go home I escape with the guys for a couple of hours every time I can. We go and smoke a joint, talk about life, look at the girls. Sometimes I build romantic stories in my head, movie scenes where we just hold hands and laugh, without a worry in our minds. We kiss like teenagers and she jumps in my arms, crossing her legs around my waist, and I turn and turn with her in my arms, her hair flying around, and she doesn't frown, and she doesn't protest, she just laughs and kisses me on the lips, her tongue searching for my tongue, and – hum – yeah, sometimes the movie in my head goes on quite far and it's like I'm with Najib and Qasim again, trying to hide the bump in my trousers.

I try to give Naghma some love. I mean, I care for her. I really do. Maybe I do even love her in a way. Every once in a while, I knock at her door, climb in her bed, and make love to her. Sometimes I kiss her, when she's put too much ginger in the karahi. But most of the time it's just kind of cold. She turns off the light and

I put on a condom. We decided together on the condom thing. We're not ready. Well… she's ready, she's been for years; but I'm not. According to our culture, we should procreate. My parents tell me every day "When are you giving us a grandson? It's time you care about your offspring, son!" Her parents curse me every day too. "Look what you're doing to our Naghma! You're wasting her time! Thirty past and no babies. What if she gets too old?" I keep telling myself that there's time. Plenty of time. The truth is, I'm scared. I'm scared they'll grow up in a world at war. I'm scared they'll see their home country being torn apart by remotely controlled death angels killing from above, imposing their merciless justice on us.

Us. I'm saying "us" as if I were still one of them; but look at me: my shirts smell of cologne and my hands of antibacterial soap. They wouldn't even recognize me "back home". I still say "back home" when I talk to people. I guess it's easier. Sometimes I go out with the boys for a Corona or a Mojito. Naghma doesn't know I drink alcohol. Nobody in my family knows. They'll never know; it would cause too much of a mess. So I go out and I start talking with some girl. For a couple of hours I embrace the illusion of a normal American life. They always ask: "Where are you from?" All of them. I speak as an American, dress as an American, drink as an American, but my nose always betrays me. "Where are you from?" – they'd ask. "America" – I'd say. "But where are you from *originally*" – inevitably follows. "Pakistan" I'd answer already expecting the grand speech about socio-politics in Pakistan and "what do you think of the Valentine's day protests?" and "Aren't these drones awful?" So here you go. Half of my life I spent in America, but it seems my nose will forever forbid me to be *from here*. I guess that's all right anyway. I never felt American either. Not sure what I feel like actually. Neither East nor West, I belong to two cultures and I belong to none.

I contemplate my life as somebody else's life: a couple of friends who get me, a tiny badass scar on the left side of my face, where they'd punched me that far-far-away night on the metro. I earn more money in a month than the whole of Chargulli, yet I keep saving and saving because I got parents who taught me right. I keep a pile of articles, books and pictures about Italy stashed away in a file cabinet at work. I haven't seen Italy. So I drive an expansive Alfa Romeo 167 dressed in red carmine and classy black leather. I drive it for hours listening to old flamenco melodies of a once-happy life I'll never get back. In the guitar's tremolos, I feel the pain of the gypsies, people with so many roots that they've lost them all. People from the East lost in the West. How I understand them!

I am free falling and it feels fantastic. I want it never to end. Or better said, it could all end right now, and it would be perfect. I could slam into the ground, smash my bones to pieces, and that would be fine. I got nothing to lose, just so much weight from which to free myself.

I am flying, feeling like a superhero. As if I were sensing my imminent death, flashbacks run through my mind. I think about Najib, but why? Images of my childhood start to resurface. I suddenly remember the long summers and the taste of the sugarcanes' juice in my mouth. I feel the sun slapping my back and the dust brushing my hair. I don't know why, I remember Najib in particular, and especially that one day of late summer when he had turned into the star of Chargulli. I had hurt my ankle – I don't remember how. Some mischief we must have been doing with the gang... It wasn´t much of a gang, really, just the three of us: Qasim, Najib, and I. But at the time we thought of ourselves as cowboys and the village was our battling field.

That day, Najib was ecstatic – I remember clearly now. I had been stuck at home for my foot and nothing was left to steal, no apples, no chickens. So Najib had decided to dedicate himself to his passion: motorbikes.

He had helped his father in the mechanical shop all morning although it was too hot to even move. He liked working with his father. It made him feel like a man, touching the greasy engines of dirty motorbikes. In no time, he would become black with oil and grease, a big line of dirt crossing his forehead where he had swept the tears of sweat. Once a month, his father would travel to Peshawar and bring back a dozen old eroded motorbikes, those slim ones with pedals you had to use going up hills. You could hear those machines paapapapapaaat around the city, carrying up to four passengers, zigzagging around the donkeys, their driver proud like a peacock. Najib was only twelve years old then, but he already knew everything about those moppets. He knew how to screw the wheels up but not too tight to give some fluidity to the movement – a much-needed asset in the chaotic streets of nearby Peshawar. For families he would pump the wheels a little bit more to allow for the extra-charge. For young men, he would spend time polishing the metal and making it bright as he knew they wanted to impress. For boys, he would cure the brakes, as they always tended to go too fast, pirouetting in the sand and throwing themselves from heights. Najib could learn everything about a moppet from the only vroom of its engine, from the clicketee of its pedals, from the resistance of its brakes. He had also found a way to change the sound of the horn. He loved scaring donkeys with high-pitch whistles or rallying the gang with a long deep blow.

Most of the bikes were brought from Iran and India to Karachi, but that morning Najib had just finished bringing to life a Japanese Honda CG 125, model of 1983. His dad had bought it in Karachi one month earlier and had given it to Najib to repair on his own. For a month Najib had worked like a poor devil, bending the metal, painting, taking off the rust, treating the iron against the mildew… he had even bought fine leather to cover the seat and a *taweez* to hang on the handlebars and protect the driver from incidents. God if he needed that *taweez*! Najib had one obsession he had taken from his elder brother: stunt riding. In those years, Najib's brother was known in the whole of Chargulli for doing The Superman.

I suddenly realize that I do not remember his brother's name. Actually, I consigned to oblivion most of those names from my *other* life. Our neighbors, our teachers… but suddenly – alone in that immensity, the cars on the streets below me growing bigger and bigger – every single face comes back to my mind. To my surprise, I can recall in details the light on their face as they watched Najib getting ready for his very first Superman.

The Superman consisted in raising the motorcycle to its posterior wheel, and holding onto it from the handlebars, legs spread behind and body straight up above the road. It gave the impression the driver was flying over the road, pulled by the bike raised straight up on one wheel. Another favorite was the Donkey Wheelie, front wheel up to the vertical, the rider standing straight, ass on the back seat, feet dragging just one cm above the ground. His brother was only fifteen and was immensely respected by all of Chargulli's kids for his boldness. His mother always beat the hell out of him whenever she would get to know about those death-defying exercises, but he didn't care. He would take the stick and cry and promise never to do it again, but the next day he would be back on the road, exhorting the crowd, leaping and prancing on the bitumen. Najib had begged him many time to lend him his Atlas Honda CG 125 – a Made-in-Pakistan bike with stickers plugged on each side of the machine – and teach him, but Mr. Superman always refused. Now Najib was ready to exhibit his machine, a Made-in-Japan creature (the summit of exoticism) that would no doubt get him the big guys and young ladies' attention. He was riding it straight up, concentrating not to let his nerves take over, crushing the hand bars as to prevent his hands from shaking. Of course, it went without saying that more than hurting himself, he was afraid to destroy his precious machine. And I, who was watching on the side, standing on my one good foot, was already dreaming of the many purposes it could serve the following summer, when the days would grow longer again and the fields would fill up with watermelons, sugarcanes, and juicy apples. I was already building up evasion plans in my mind, riding the bike behind Najib, my hands filled with stolen goodies.

Finally, Najib shoot off, making the motor roar like a ferocious tiger. He took up to speed, raised up and tried to pull the front wheel up. Meanwhile everybody was laughing, taking bets on whether he would even manage to raise the bike to the vertical. The front wheel got off the ground by about five centimeters, but Najib was too weak. Everybody was already losing interest. The youngest person ever to manage the Superman was Najib's brother at thirteen. Najib was twelve and his entire muscular strength consisted of two pathetic barely-showing biceps. He did not stand a chance. Suddenly shouts fused from the crowd. Najib´s front wheel was turning freely high above the ground and the boy was starting to find his balance. Everybody was shouting encouragements. Only Najib's brother was keeping silent, in no way interested in seeing his little brother steal his title. But Najib was unstoppable. He was already placing his feet on the seat, and searching a way to abandon them to the pavement. It took him a few trials. He'd run after the bike for a few seconds but could never decide himself to pull his weight down. He was too worried about keeping the bike straight. The crowd was shouting louder and louder, pumping up courage into Najib's veins. Najib had already completed two circles around the village and returned again to where I could see him (me, the only one who couldn't run after him like all the other kids). Just then – as if to impress me and nobody else - did he flush his feet backward and let them drag a couple inches above the ground, flying like a superhero behind his shiny black Honda CG 125.

As my feet touch the ground I stumble a few steps trying to find my balance. The parachute pulls me back just as I'm about to fall head first in the mud. Instead, I get kicked down on my butt, feet up, rolling backward over my head, and smacked down, nose deep in the mud just the same. I don't care. Nothing can upset me today. I get up and look up at the sky. I watch that immensity of deep blue I just challenged. I am the superhero! I want to go again. Again and again. I want to spend the rest of my life throwing myself in the void, defying danger, being weightless.

Back at the base, I look at my cell-phone. 6pm. Seventeen missed calls from home. Ten from Naghma, six from my parents, one from my sister. Nobody knows I'm here. Nobody knows what I just did. I'm nine again.

Against my will, despite the half-hour of pure joy, despite my ears still buzzing from the stern winds up there, anger fills me up as I'm looking at the missed calls' light beeping on the screen. Why don't they leave me alone? Why don't they let me be? Haven't I given enough already? Naghma, sweet unbearable Naghma! I tried so hard to make her happy. I tried it all.

The day she finally arrived in the States, I went to get her from the airport with flowers in my hands and a sign that read "پخير". Pakheyr: welcome. I had not seen her in seven years, not since we'd pronounced those fatidic "yes" in front of the mullah. She had put on weight and smelled so heavily of curry I had to open the car's window despite the chilly late March breeze. We both tried very hard to make it work at the beginning. She'd cook delicious pots from "back home" and I'd show her the city, the little bright houses with well-kept gardens of Dupont Circle. I'd take her out to Adams Morgan where I'd feed her exotic dishes from Ethiopia, Mongolia, Spain… In April I took her to the Cherry Blossom, then in the summer I invited her to kayak on the Potomac and enjoy lemonade on the Waterfront.

Most people think DC is boring – a city of bureaucrats, FBI

agents and terribly serious white people. But they don't know DC. They haven't spent time exploring its dark allies, sitting at the bookstores sipping on a mocha-latte, or dancing salsa on the tables of Café Citron till the wee hours of the morning. I wanted to share with her everything I loved about DC. So I drove with her everywhere from Rock Creek Park on the North to Alexandria on the South, and from Georgetown on the East even all the way to allegedly dangerous Anacostia on the West. At the beginning she'd mouth Ooohs and Aaaahs whenever she'd see or taste something new. She'd ask about the monuments and jump in surprise when some crazy beggar would shout "God bless you!" Yet her enthusiasm came to an end together with the summer. By the winter, numbed by the cold and her loneliness, she was spending all of her time at home, dedicating herself to finding a way to bring her family to the States. She'd refuse to speak in English and would only interact with Pakistani women from her mosque.

Eventually I grew tired of trying and just let her be. A year later – at her request – her parents left Pakistan and moved in with us. What could I do? I allowed it, just as I have allowed everything else to happen to me: a passive spectator of my own life.

The phone rings once more. I let it go to voicemail. I just flew! I just defied gravity. So, the hell with them! It's time for me. 2012: the end of the world, right? The new consciousness, the Mayas, and all that. C'mon! May this world end! May a new one begin, I don't care! I'm already speeding up the highway, zigzagging in between the Prius and the SUVs. Good versus Evil. Believers versus hoarders. Spirituality versus reality shows. Ain't that funny?

Without thinking I get to the airport. I plant myself in front of the destinations board, vaguely hoping to see Islamabad somewhere in the list. I am ready to entrust myself over to destiny. I walk over to one of the desks tree-lining the airport's vast departure hall.

- "Put me on the next flight available, please."
- "Where to, sir?"
- "Anywhere. Whichever leaves first."

She throws an eye over the counter to search for luggage. She doesn´t seem very happy to realize I've got nothing. She looks at my passport more attentively this time.

- "What is the reason of your trip, sir?"
- "Holiday!"

I smile at her but she responds with an uneasy frown. She picks up the phone and calls in her superior. I suddenly realize what's going on, what it must look like. My name, my nose. Me with my fucking name and my fucking nose and no luggage, no destination.

- "Never mind, miss. I know what you're thinking. I'm not a terrorist. I'm just a tired US citizen in need of a vacation. But I was born in Pakistan. Pakistani people don't take vacations, do they? They only make bombs, right? All day long! Bombs, everywhere!"

- "Sir…"

She's as livid as I'm red. I need to calm down fast. Pakistani-born people don't have a right to get angry. They just have the right to shut up.

- "It's okay. I won't bother you anymore. Can I have my passport back, please?"

She suspiciously hands over my passport, looking even more anxious. She seems to be scanning behind my shoulder for a security agent or a border patrol. I retreat. I haven't forgotten that beating in the metro. It's been ten years but not much has change, has it?

I return to my car in a hurry. I don't want anybody questioning. What would they know? They can't understand. They have no idea. They don't know what it means to be a prisoner of your own life. They don't know that a name doesn't make you a terrorist, anger does. And I'm not angry. I'm just a frustrated US citizen with a big nose, in need of a vacation away from his life.

I abandon myself to the expensive leather of my Alfa Romeo, arrogant proof of my success and good taste. I feel like taking a nap.

Going to sleep and never waking up, but my stupidly smart phone vibrates in my pocket, again and again. I let it go to voice mail, again. I want to throw the damn phone away, but I've been programmed. I've been programmed to listen to my phone, push its buttons the way it likes it. The message sign is beeping on the screen and I can't help it. I must check it. At least the message. I hesitate for a second, certain it will scream my wife's reprimands, but it is stronger than me. I gotta push the read button – make the beeping light stop. The message pops up and I read it once, then again, then six, seven, thirty times!

"Sameer, I'm pregnant. Please come home."

I'm running through the hospital corridors. There's a problem with the baby. I left the stash of paperwork on my desk, left the computer on and all the programs running. I'm not even sure I turned off the car engine randomly parked in the parking lot. Why is this hospital so big? So many corridors. So many doors. I can't stop thinking in a loop. Everything is going to be okay. If it's a girl we'll call her Maya, she will like music and falling asleep in my lap in front of the TV. She will be at the door waiting for me when I come home from work, or she will be jumping on the sofa dancing a bit clumsily to Qawwali melodies and tunes of the Gyspy Kings. A child of both worlds, she will grow up to be smart and independent. Maya she will have the chance her mother never had: she'll fall in love. I'll make sure she does. I'll make sure she gets a say.

When I get to the door where my wife is supposed to be consulted, a nurse informs me that she's been taken into surgery. My head spins. I let myself fall into an armchair. I can't breathe. All I can think about is my baby being torn apart by the scalpels and the clamps. Oh God please don't let my baby die!

I try to reason. If it's a girl we'll call her Maya, and if it's a boy we'll call him Hewad: "homeland". Pakistan will be his home and the United States will be his home. He won't have a big nose like me, but a proper one, one that gets unnoticed, one that white bullies won't want to beat up. He will be a little devil, just like me, but he will like bikes, just like Najib. I'll watch him grow and it will be like freefalling every time. For every meter square of bitumen he'll have to step, I will create for him playgrounds of sand and dust. I'll teach him to hunt chickens and cut sugarcanes. I don't know how. Here there's no chickens and no sugarcanes. The only chickens I've seen since I got here were all beheaded and tucked in plastic. But I'll figure it out. If he survives, I'll do anything.

I try to remember the past seven months, since I sat down in my car, numbed, reading over and over that text message. How stupid had I been! I nearly left without a word. Now everything's changed. A stupid condom broke and everything changed, just like that. Just like that I became a dad and I was scared as shit; scared but happy, ridiculously happy. Just like that, I didn't care anymore that she turns off the light when we make love so that I wouldn't see the rolls on her hips. I didn't even care so much anymore that her mother spends all of her time at our place, always commenting on my haircut, always interrogating me "you've been to the mosque today?" "You asked God for His protection?" "God will give if you ask, but you have to ask with your heart! Now go pray. Hush. Go!" She never stopped blabbering yet just like that not even her shrieking voice bothered me anymore.

The minutes go by so slow and nobody comes out. My baby's in there and I am blinded. All I can do is pray. So I am praying like mad, asking God with all my heart for my baby to be okay. Right now I am making any kind of pacts with God so that he doesn't take my baby. "Let it live and I'll never drink nor smoke again. I'll make a pilgrimage to Al Masjid al Haram. I'll travel to Saudi Arabia on my bare feet, I won't eat for a month, I'll sell my Alfa Romeo, I'll give my clothes to the poor, but please, please don't take my baby!"

The surgeon comes out; some blood has spilled onto his blue scrubs. He smiles at me and extends a hand that is so graceful and neat I'm afraid to squeeze it.

- "Mr. Ahmadi?"
- "Doctor."

My hand is shaking inside his.

- "They're fine. Both of them (*Al-Hamdulillah!* resonates like a bell in my head). Your wife suffered from internal bleeding, but we were able to stop it. Fortunately your little girl is strong. She held up just fine."
- "A girl? I'm having a girl?"
- "Yes sir. You're having a healthy little girl."

I hug him as my savior. I hug him like I had not hugged anybody in a very long time. Only seven months ago I was getting ready to die, escape, disappear, whatever to save my egoistic self from my miserable fate. How a baby changes your life, it's terrifying. The relief knocks me off my feet, bringing tears to my eyes. My heart fills up with love for Naghma, for she has given me a child, my child. Little Maya who will be so strong and beautiful. Little Maya who will love music – just like me – and juggle with numbers – just like her mum. I can't wait to see her, her tiny little hands, her wrinkled little feet.

Naghma is sleeping with one hand resting on her round belly, the other loosely clutched on the side of her head. She looks so dark in the white bed, covered in white sheets. Her heavy black hair is spreading on the white pillow like a tarantula. I stand by her side. Looking at her belly. I wish I had x-ray vision, just like Superman, so I could see that tiny creature growing up inside. She already has feet and arms, and eyes, and a miniscule heart beating inside her miniscule chest. She doesn't have hair yet; her organs are not yet fully developed. She has palmed hands where tiny little fingers are slowly being carved. She looks like a jellybean. My jellybean. I put my hand on Naghma's hand. For the first time I feel like hugging her, because she's got my baby inside her. She's got my life inside her. How could I ever think of leaving her?

When I was young – just a little boy – my *naani* died. She was ill, nothing they could do about it. That very morning I had been playing with the boys and while running – at the very moment she passed away just a few houses down – I fell and hurt my knee pretty bad. Shazmina found me crying in the middle of the street. She took me in her arms and carried me towards the house, patting my hair and while rocking me she kept repeating softly, "*ma batchey*, you've got to be strong. You've got to be strong". I watched my *naani* lay lifeless in the bed. Her salt-and-paper hair was spreading on the white pillow like an old tarantula. I put my scratched up tiny boy hand on top of her hands, joined together on her empty belly. I was hurting inside and out, feeling miserable. I told my mum how angry I was with God for he was giving me a hard time. Shazmina took me aside and sat with me on the shapeless mattress, holding me tight against the warmth of her chest. Her hijab had fallen backwards on her shoulders, revealing her dark patted hair. She took my hand in both her hands and started speaking very softly.

- "Sameer, *ma batchey*. I know life seems tough right now, and there will be many more times like that. You must never lose faith. Remember that I love you, and your dad loves you, and so does God. Whenever you feel that everything is dark and that life is only throwing challenges at you, then something really great and bright is coming. And if you ever get very successful and everything seems to go your way, then stay humble and tough, *ma batchey*, because God is getting ready to test you, to make sure you're worthy. You don't show your worth in good times. Good times are easy. Good times are like sleeping at night. They are necessary, your life depends on them, but they don't get you anywhere. Bad times are like being awake: only by living and fighting can you grow, learn, and become a better person. And then one day, you'll be a dad too, and you will sit by your child's bed and tell him the very same thing. You will tell him never to be afraid, never to give up. You will take his hands when he is sad and keep him down to earth when he is very happy. And you will discover that life always gets better, because now your *naani* is watching over you, nagging God, making sure that he keeps some good surprises for you at the end of the running line."

Outside the hospital, rain is sizzling, blessing me. Some people pass by but they don't even look at me. They go by their life, hastily going from an ill parent to a warm house, a cat purring by the fire grate, a dozen cupcakes in the oven. From life to death and from death to life. Outside, on the other side of earth, 7153.2 miles from here, the sun is burning cold. Winter is already plunging its claws into the hard soils of Chargulli. Maybe at this exact moment Najib is playing with his boy. He must be 10 years old by now. I wonder if he knows about the Supermans and the Donkey Wheelies. Qasim still owns his father's shop, I'm sure of it. He was so agile. He must have found a way to save it from the ravages of war. It must be even thriving now: soaps, light bulbs, lipstick for the ladies, second-hand shoes, handy tools, and who knows what sort of illegal stuff he might be selling too!

Qasim sent me a letter once, six years ago. "You remember when we used to steal that old naani's chickens?" he was asking in his letter. Boy, if I remembered! "My son, he is just the same. Seven years old and already hiding everywhere! The old naani found him hiding among her freshly washed bedclothes. She got so surprised that she suffered a heart attack and died on the spot. Can you believe that? The old nag was like ninety-two and my boy killed her! We went to her funeral and everybody was there. Najib and his four kids. Yes, four! Crazy, right? I stopped after three. It's hard to feed that many mouths, you know. So? What's up with you, Amriki? You coming back home any time soon?"

I answered a couple months later with some generalities. "Life's good" is all I found to say about myself. God! I wish I could write to him now. Tell him that I've got a baby girl on the way, tell him I'm gonna be a dad too. Finally something I can tell him without feeling guilty and estranged. He never answered back again though. It's been six years. I don't even know if he's alive. I never tried reaching out again. So caught up as I was in my studies, my job, my Pathan duties, my Yankee shame. I told the boys here, of course; but it's not the same. Qasim and Najib, they are my childhood memories, tying me back to my homeland. I've been here so long, some images of Chargulli have started to fade away. The names, some faces, that old naani's scent: I don't remember it. It gets messed up with other names, faces, and scents. Does that chicken karahi really taste like back home? And does that guy at work remind me of Chargulli's baker, after all?

I get into my car, take off the flamenco music USB key and ramble through the gloves' compartment for an old CD I hadn't listen to in a while. I put it in its slot, turn the car keys and listen to the motor purr as the first notes rise:

MaiN azal se bandaa-e-ishq huuN

muhhe zuhd-o-kufr kaa Gham nahiiN

mere sar ko dar teraa mil gayaa

mujhe ab talaash-e-haram nahiiN.

The heavily tattooed bold man behind the counter sends me to a glass cubicle in the back of the internet café. I grab the dirty handset, which may have once been white, and stick it between my ear and my shoulder. I dial the number with great care and then just listen quietly as it rings and rings, repeatedly. After six rings somebody finally picks up with a raucous cough filled with dust and cheap tobacco.

- "Alô? (Arkh kh kh) Alo? Salaam. Zama num Samir de. Alo?"
- "Kha! Kha!"
- "Qasim, lotfan. Qasim Khan."

I hear the noise of the handset being left on the table and a few steps fading away. I'm waiting, watching the dollars add up, dime by dime: $3.50, $3.60… It has already reached $7.80 when finally I hear some noise again.

- "Alo?"
- "Qasim?"
- "Sameer?"

I feel the emotion grabbing my guts, rushing through my body all the way to my eyes. Shit! I'm nearly crying! I erase those nascent tears with the back on my hand. It's been so long. Just now I realized I had been scared. Since I last saw him, so much has happened. September 11 happened. The war, the drones, the kids… Naghma. Everything happened. An entire new world order has bestowed its rules upon us, since our last short correspondence. I though he may have been injured – or… dead. The sound of his voice is like a detonator, pushing air outside my body, bludgeoning in my mouth, tearing my throat. What has happened to me? My friends could have been dead and all I thought about all these years has been me. Myself. My bad luck, my annoying boss, my slightly overweight wife.

- "Sameer? Is that you?"

I try to answer but all that spurs out is a giant sob.

- "Ta sanga yee?"
- "Sameer! What happened? Are you… crying?"
- "No. I mean yes. I mean… I thought you might be…"
- "Dead?"
- "Kha."
- "I'm ok Sameer. Najib is ok too. We manage."
- "And your kids?"
- "They are little devils, just like us back then."

I smile and I cry, tears run down my cheeks.

- "What about you Sameer?"
- "I'm going to be a dad. I'm having a little girl."
- "That's good Sameer. That's really good."

I can hear his tired smile, the moist in his voice.

- "Qasim. I'm sorry you're there, suffering, and I'm here, living the good life. I wish… I wish I could help you guys. I wish I could get you to come here."
- "Shut up Sameer. We don't need no Yankee's help."

I smile in between my tears. Qasim sure hasn't lost his verve.

- "I'm no Yankee, y'allah!"
- "You sure are! I bet you're driving a big shot car now, aren't you?"

I look at my shining Alfa parked outside the call center.

- "Shit, man!"

Qasim laughs. It's a raucous laugh. It doesn't sound so good, but I'll take it anyway: it's the laugh of a warrior.

- "Listen, big shot! You don't worry about getting us there, ok? I ain't wanna become a damn disadapted like you, dude."
- "Disadapted? Whatcha talking about? I ain't disadapted!"
- "Yeah, right! Watcha gonna call your girl anyway?"
- "Maya."
- "Maya. That's a yankee name!"
- "Hey!"
- "I'm kidding *stoopid*! It's a good name. I like it."
- "Jerk!"

- "Hey, Sameer. Don't get her all confused like you, alright? There ain't gonna be any "back home" for her. You know that, right?"
- …
- "Gotta go. Just come visit once in a while, dude. We miss you, you know."
- "Kha. I miss you too, guys."
- "Khuda Hafiz."
- "Khuda Hafiz, Qasim."

I get out the call center feeling upset. Why did Qasim have to ruin it for me? Disadapted? That's not even a word! I tuck my hands in my pockets and kick the gravel with the tip of my feet, just like I used to when I was a kid and my mother would call me in for dinner, and all I wanted was to play with the gang just a little while longer. Only now my naked feet are trapped inside 200-bucks' worth polished shoes. In a movement of rage I kick them off, throwing them far away. Then I start walking proudly towards my "big shot" car but the gravel hurts my feet and I hobble along like a clown trapped in a cage filled with scorpions. Even my feet are against me. I used to harness any path with those feet, barefoot in the dust, barefoot in the mountains, barefoot everywhere like a goat! But I'm left with delicate feet that cannot stand freedom no more.

Humiliated, I grab my shoes back and return to the security of a car that half the men in Chargulli would kill to drive even just once, including Qasim. "*Stoopid*". That's how we used to call the adults, as kids. Well stoopid him! What does he know about my life? What does he know about Yankees? I'm no Yankee!

I drive down south, take a turn on Route 64. I've got a couple of hours before the sun sets. I rush down the highway, now going southeast, allowing my feelings to flow freely, letting them smear all over the bitumen, the trees, all over the clearing sky above my head. I pass residential houses with brick walls, with proper gardens, the grass cut short, the bushes trimmed. Nothing is out of place. The cars stop at the stop signs. The children walk quietly on the sidewalk. Everything is the opposite of Chargulli: sounds, smells, rhythms. Here everything is quiet, scents of the rain mixing with the iodine of the ocean. The Chesapeake Bay appears on my left, as I cross the Hampton Roads Beltway. The panorama opens to infinity. Greyish ducks slide silently on the greyish waters of the Bay, leaving behind silky wrinkles. The world goes by slowly in Virginia, while in the Chargulli of my souvenirs scents of spices tickle the donkeys' nostrils, causing them to bray desperately, covering the honking of the cars and door-less trucks. Kids run in between the cars and bicycles, followed by streams of cusses and raised fists. Everything moves erratically yet joyfully and I, too, participate to that chaos, chasing street cats, jumping on walls, and running after Qasim and Najib, our naked feet bouncing free over sand, stones and donkeys' excrements.

I let those memories slide behind me, disappear over the horizon's line. I offer those memories to the vast universe, the lakes, the oceans. I offer them to everybody and everything. I depose my story at God's feet, as an offering, my thank-you gift to Him. I watch over the Atlantic Ocean, perfectly still, perfectly peaceful. I let my body cool, becoming weightless as the kilometers bring me peace and resignation.

I park in the empty parking lot and climb down the stairs to Virginia Beach. I take off my shoes (calmly this time), roll up my trousers and plunge my toes into the sand till they're covered in it. It is cold, fresh, soothing. I breathe in the sea breeze. The sun is already tipping into the water like a giant cookie being dipped into milk by the hand of God. I bathe in the giant cookie's light, cooling down. Do you feel that, little Maya? Do you feel that light shining upon you from your belly crib? Do you hear me calling your name? You're not even born yet, already I'd die for you. Already I feel jealous of all the men in your future. I feel scared of all the thorns and bumps, all the fights, all the battles to come. Will you laugh at your old father when I can't make right from wrong? Will you understand me when I teach you the words of Islam, those very same words I barely even remember? Will you mock me when I instruct you to fall in love, "but don't you dare drinking alcohol or eating pork!"? Will you pity me when I put you to sleep with stories of my childhood, the tricks with the gang, the old naani's chickens? Will you believe me when I tell you that I was born with dust beneath my feet?

May this be your land of opportunities, *ma batchey*! May this be your land! There won't be any "back home" for you and maybe it's just as good. Your father is a disadapted, *ma batchey*. Neither East nor West, neither from here nor from there. Does it matter? I felt so lost without an etiquette. I let others convince me it was important. Fundamental, even! Etiquettes are mirages, the illusory comfort of belonging to a group, the purest expression of cowardice. But you, *ma batchey*, will embrace none and all of them. You will be from everywhere and nowhere and you will carry with you the fantastic heritage of all cultures, of all lights.

I walk over to the ocean, letting the waves lick my feet, washing the sand off, washing the scars of every path travelled off. Of my entire village, I was the luckiest: the one who won the lottery! I lived the American dream and made it. From dust to sand, from East to West, I became the lucky bearer of two cultures, the lucky owner of that new world where you, *ma batchey*, will learn to live beyond definitions.

Wave after wave, the ocean carries my past away. I forget the war, I forget the insults. I forget the drones, I forget Qasim's raucous voice. I forget the suspicious look on that woman's face at the airport. I forget every time I was called "Al Qaeda" and asked to go "back home". I forget the sound of that word, "terrorist", resonating in my ears like a bell leading me to the scaffold erected by the people I thought of as mine. I even forget that night in the metro, my father's demise and my mother's tears. I forget it all to make space for a thousand new memories, happy memories of little Maya's journey into this life.

I free myself from all borders, all definitions, and I feel light, mind and body finally at peace. I see Maya trotting besides me, jumping over the waves, laughing with a laugh so clear it makes every other sound disappear. In the pinks and golds of the dying sun, I open my arms, wide, like wings, and let the light impregnate me, abandoning myself to the overwhelming feeling of pure happiness.

And so I win.

8- ODE AD UN POVERO CRISTO

Rome, Italy, 2012

-   "Ue, Nico, guardi che bionna bambaciona!"

I search in the direction indicated by the raised arm of my colleague, pointing shamelessly at a voluptuous young girl in a tight T-shirt. She is sitting on the short wall opposite the Lungotevere Raffaello Sanzio. I observe her for a few seconds, reading her voluminous novel – probably Dostoyevsky (although she might just as well be reading the Twilight trilogy, dreaming to sink her teeth in some pale boy's neck, but I prefer to believe that true culture has not died just yet). She is biting her bottom lip in a cute way, the fuchsia of her lipstick perfectly matching the fuchsia of her black-and-fuchsia bag, black-and-fuchsia shoes, black-and-fuchsia shirt, an explosion of black and fuchsia all carefully calculated to result in a noticeable yet not overbearing proof of her good style. I switch my scrutiny to an old woman sitting just a few trees down the Tiber. She's wearing a red polka-dot flanelle shirt and a marine blue skirts that brushes her knees. She is reading too, a much thinner book, I'm thinking poetry. For some reason Anais Nin comes to my mind. Maybe because despite her initiated decrepitude she radiates the same energy I have seen on women after they'd been taken by the ecstasy of sexual pleasure. The heat she exalts reminds me of how long it's been since I gave a woman an orgasm. It's been 13 months and 3 days exactly. I didn't count. I didn't have to count. My body has been doing the counting for me. Every day adding up like an old prisoner scratches with his dirty nails the walls of his prison cell: one-two-three-four shaky straight bars and a fifth one running deep across.

The old lady puts on a tiny hat crowned with what I suppose may have been bright pink roses once – long ago. It must look pretty sad, but in my eyes she shines like a beautiful antique to be touched only very carefully. She tiptoes slowly along the river, stops at a dustbin hanging there, on a tired pole. I thought for a minute she might throw in her tiny book. She must have not liked it. But instead she plunges her frail hand in the mouth of the bin and takes upon scavenging its bowels. I look away, resolved not to care. I do not need another sad story today. I need some good news, for once. I draw a last drag from my rolled-up cigarette. Looking for a minute at the yellow stains on my fingers reminds me once more that I should really stop that shit. Frustrated, I draw yet another drag from the disgusting cadaver's butt. The image sends me back – again – to a time when "that shit" had been my only company, for weeks, when sitting on the mildewed floor of a cell in Jalalabad. There had been no passionate kiss that time, no surprise romance. Just a famished guard who was as much of a prisoner as I was. He felt sorry for me, because I'd been arrested trying to save people like him, smuggling them over the Afghan border, along the feared Multan-Lahore Road, all the way to Peshawar where they'd thank me with an exhausted handshake and disappear forever in the growling crowd of sheep, donkeys, *taratating* bitty boxes, unapproachable women and haggard men. The guard would provide me with rice and cigarette butts. Sometimes he'd stay and chat me up a bit. He'd keep me company with stories of his family, of who he used to be, what he used to do, before the Talibans, before the Yankees, "before everything went so nuts that they'd start fighting for a bunch of rocks and stones". Weaken up by the lack of light and vitamins, I did not have the strength to explain about the natural gas running below the rocks and how all those greedy powers seek more what is underneath than above. He knew it all too well, anyway.

Anyway. I don't really care for all those memories. My boss is calling me from the kitchen. I throw in the gutter the piece of filter and burnt paper I'm still holding in between my tired yellow fingers. I drag myself to the kitchen.

- "You gotta start smoking less and working harder boy, I got no room for slackers here!"

I nod. I want to slap that jerk in the face. He thinks he's so important with his restaurant on the Lungotevere. He thinks he runs the world because he shook Berluska's hand once. He gotta brag about it all the time too. I want to slap him but I do nothing. I grab a not-too-clean towel and start sweeping the steaming cups straight out of the washing machine. As he leaves the room though, I grab a leftover piece of pizza and a take-away coffee semifreddo in a plastic bowl. Hiding the food in my apron, I run across the street. The hobo lady is now scavenging the next bin. I offer her the cold pizza and the day-old desert. I find myself pathetic with my ridiculous offering, but she doesn't seem to care. She looks at me with gratitude, extends her long gnarled fingers and swiftly grabs her loot. I don't give her time to thank me; I'm already back in the restaurant where everybody is sluggishly getting ready for the evening shift.

The heavy wooden clock marks 2am. Finished work. Played my part and took orders. Mostly couples tonight, and Tomaso, the writer who comes eat his Margherita every time he returns from a trip: a summit in Shanghai, a conference in Dubai.

- "I just came back from Istanbul, doing research for my next novel" he announces excitedly. "Istanbul is amazing! You wouldn't believe it!"
- "It really is, indeed."
- "Oh, you know Istanbul? When were you there?"

Tomaso always tries to get me to talk, tells me my story should be told. I keep refusing on the ground that I'm already writing it, but of course he's not buying it.

- "Common Nico, come have a drink. You and I, we can tell the youth, change the way people think and understand the world. Tell them the truth about this damn crisis that is no crisis at all. Tell them it's just a show put on by the beasts. They think if they get the play going till the end they'll win, but you and I, we know they'll just end up dying on stage, like Moliere, a much better show for everybody to enjoy. We gotta tell them there's hope, Nico. Otherwise what will happen? They won't go vote, they won't fight, they'll let Italy fade away. The world needs hope. With my columns and your stories, we can give them hope, Nico. Look at this guy, Stéphane Hessel, who wrote about getting outraged. He got the people out on the streets, he did it. We can make the Indignados movement grow, make it stronger. We ought to, Nico!"

- "I don't care, Tomaso! Not now. It's Friday night and the youth is out to dance, Tomaso. Let me be young still, let me go be an idiot for a little while longer."

Before I can reach the door, Mr. Boss calls me from across the room and gestures me to come over with his greasy index curbed towards him. Even his index is smug.

- "Sì?"
- "Nico, look: I'm sorry. I gotta let you go. You know… times are hard. I have to do some restructuration, make some sacrifices. Believe me, I hate it as much as you do, I wish I could keep you, really. It's really nothing you did… Contingencies, that's all."
- "…"
- "But you don't worry, boy. You'll be okay. I'll write a good recommendation for you, okay? You know what? I'm gonna recommend you to my cousin! He's got a restaurant near the Foro Romano. The Foro Romano, ain't that great, boy? C'mon, don't be mad. Look, if you feel like yelling at me, go ahead, I understand. Whatever you need to get you to feel better."

Stunned by his fawning hypocrisy, I remain frozen for a minute, realizing I had just been given "the speech". I could punch him right now. Not because he's firing me; I don't give a damn about the bloody job anyway – but because he called me "boy", with the same condescendence that those haughty soldiers at the Qulandia checkpoint. Sometimes the men I carried across the Afghan-Pakistani border called me "boy" too. "Ya halek! Staa num de, halek?" they'd ask, trying to befriend me, hoping for a discount; but the tone was soft. It never bothered me. The Israeli soldiers, though… I once spit in one's face because he called me boy. He thanked me flushing the butt of his M-16 across my face. I laughed at him.

Where has my bravery gone today? Time has killed the rebel in me, or was it the civilized world? Since I came back, day after day, they've bent me. They who? Them all! Bosses, passers-by, dull executives at employment agencies.

They broke me.

I walk away. Tommaso, unaware, annoyingly optimistic, irritating cliché of the anarco-bourgeois intellectual, waves at me in a last attempt to invite me over for a chat. I ignore him and turn one last time over to my past before I disappear through the door, cold as a lifeless robot:

- "Screw you."

I wake up, still a bit drugged up. Weed and whisky. The perfect mix for a stranded man.

I try to get up but I can't. I'm too heavy. Instead I roll over to face the wall. My wall used to be white. I haven't re-painted it. Why would I paint a place that is not mine? Give that pleasure to Mister Landlord? The heater has been broken since I got here and he never returned a single of my emails about it. I place the money in his account, once a month, and that's it. I've never even seen him. So I'm not painting any damn wall, not repairing any damn heater. I will leave again one day soon anyway. I wake up in the morning and I think I'm going to leave. It's my curse, I was told. I don't know where to. I don't even care where to. A place with just sand and silence; and nothing else. Funny how I've seen most of Asia, but I've never crossed any ocean. I always stayed on safe steady ground. I draw a map in my head and throw a pin randomly. It lands in the middle of the Pacific. Sounds good to me.

The alarm cries next door. I feel like yelling at the neighbor, but I roll over once more instead. I look at my life from above, from far away from my skin. I stink of cold cigarette and there's beer stuck in my hair. I have flashbacks of the night. They get messed up with other flashbacks, from back in Istanbul. Istanbul… my graveyard. Why does it have to come back now? Right. Tommaso… *Cazzo*!

A dim ray of light across the shutters flutters on the dirty ceiling. I remember a similar morning in Istanbul, the same stink around me, the same bugging sunray shouting me there's life outside. Only back then I'm not heavy. I'm light as a puma. I turn around to see Yael sleeping next to me. Her black curls are all over her face. She's perfectly round and tanned while the months in Jalalabad's jail have suck the color out of me, turning me into a sack of chalky bones.

Jalalabad... After three months without hearing from me, she crosses the Blue Mountains where she is working for yet another of her stupid NGOs. Utopic Yael. Always working to save the world. She moves the whole of Kabul to find me, gigantic tiny Yael. Only I'm rotting in a humid cell and there's no track record of it. One day my guard – who's grown fond of me – tells me:

- "So, there's this girl looking for you. She even dresses as a man and goes into places where women are not allowed".
- "How do you know she's looking for me?"

I'm too weak to form a proper thought in my head and get excited.

- "She says she's looking for an Italian guy with big blue eyes. Not so many of those around here, you know. A Jewish woman turning Jalalabad upside down to find a bony draggle-tailed Italian criminal, that's something I hadn't seen yet!"

And he leaves – giggling –, excited to have something new to tell his wife and eleven kids.

I'm not sure how Yael eventually got me out. Just getting

yourself heard as a woman in Jalalabad, it's like wishing death. But my Yael she's a tigress. She growls and bites. She's a tornado more powerful than prejudices. We escaped Afghanistan together, crossing over to Pakistan like fugitives, escaping a lawless law. I knew all too well the dangers of crossing by truck. Two years of smuggling people across the border had taught me better. We went by foot, using the same dangerous mountain path as thousands and thousands of Afghan refugees before us. We reached Ghalanai in the Tribal Areas of Pakistan in less than a week. Under our feet the Meter Lan valley opened up like a giant mouth. Up above our heads, the US F-16 were raiding, maybe scanning for their next target: a military depot, Bin Laden's refuge, an innocent family's house. Who knew? After Ghalanai, we reached Shabqadar where the Pakistani patrols were chewing on gums and polishing their Beretta 92F. The new apogee of the world-famous Made-in-Italy. Handguns, machine-guns, antipersonnel land mines. State-of-the-art Made-in-Italy jewels! "Pezzi di merda, Mafiosi e' merda!" but nobody was listening. I closed my eyes, shushed down my rage, and followed into Yael's footsteps all the way to Shabqadar, then south to Peshawar where, in the bathrooms of the train station, Yael patiently washed me and shaved me. We took the train from Peshawar to Islamabad, and from Islamabad's airport straight to wherever. Wherever turned out to be Istanbul, and Istanbul turned out to be a single motel room where we spent days and nights making love. Its walls were burgundy red. Its floors were made of tired parquet. It must have been pretty, once. The owner said it was built as a copy of the ancient konaks which once populated the city. They were tall wooden edifices inhabited by the riches of Istanbul. They all burnt through the ages. This one was built by an old nostalgic who died before he could step foot in it. Madame Gülnihal bought it for a few Lira and turned it into a house of cheap pleasure and depravation. If the pious man had known what his late-life dream would turn into, he would probably had burnt it to the ground. And if his old age had not killed him, the sight of his precious compilation of ahadith sitting next to a three-foot-high talentless representation of the Kamasutra's Glowing Juniper position would no doubt have done the trick. Madame Gülnihal, who despised religion in all its forms, had taken great care in conserving the late devout possessions, for the sole pleasure of desacralizing them.

In between the Qurans and the erotic portraits, we took a vibrant pleasure in being a part of the profanation. The prostitutes next door would express loudly their ecstasy, so would we. They would get Turkish sweets and tea delivered to their door, so would we. We lived of nothing but love, sweets and tea.

We went on like that for about ten days. Then one afternoon she said:

-   "I'm leaving!"
-   "Where should we go, *bimba*?"
-   "I'm going home, Nico. And I'm going alone."
-   "I don't understand."

She looks at me. Her dark eyes are so severe they pierce my skin. In her eyes I see Angela, I see the look on her face as she ran through the grapevines and the peach trees.

- "What if I had not been able to save you? What if they'd killed you?"

She caresses with the tip of her fingers the scars covering my body, one after the other. The scar on my temple, where the Israeli soldier flushed his M16. Yael was fighting Palestinian rights in Jerusalem, while I forged fake passports. A year later she followed me to Iraq, where I smuggled goods and documents from village to village. She caresses my distorted knee, memories of my escape through the rocky mountains of Iraq after my truck got raided by a bunch of soldiers. I see sadness and exhaustion flickering under the light of her unbreakable resolution. By the time her fingers reach my feet, eaten away by the humidity fungus, souvenir of Jalalabad, I know she's made her choice.

- "I'm tired Nico. I'm tired of fighting. Look at us. Look at this place. We got nothing. I'm 30 years old and I've built nothing. No family, no base, no career. My friends are getting married, they're having kids, and us? What are we doing?"
- "*Bimba*, don't say that. I can give you kids if that's what you want!"
- "I don't just want kids Nico. I want a family! Don't you understand? We spent the last ten years escaping. Ten years of

meeting in shady hotels, ten years of finding each other and escaping from each other."

- "I thought you liked it… We helped a lot of people. We saved a lot of people too. And we had a lot of fun too, didn't we?"

- "We did Nico. We sure did. But we're not young anymore. At least I'm not. I feel like a used kitchen towel. All this fighting's been useless. Palestine, Iraq, Afghanistan... We did it all, didn't we? You the handsome bad guy smuggling people across the borders, defying the law, playing with danger. Me the good girl, bringing food, raising funds, being the voice of diplomacy… What for? They're still fighting. We can never save them all. Let's face it. Out of all the families you've smuggled across borders, at your own risks, saving them from war and devastation, how many of them actually did something good with their life? How many fought, how many protested? And how many just ended up rotting in refugee camps?"

- "I don't know, *bimba*. Maybe it's true, but you… You helped a lot of people!"

- "Did I? Did I really? Tell me, who have I helped, where are they now all these people? Can't you see? It never gets better. It just shifts from one lobby to the other, rich people with rich people, power-angry vultures. Power-angry rats. Let me go home Nico! Let me rest, let me have just a normal life, a normal job! I'm sick and tired of saving a world that doesn't want to be saved."

I wanted to tell her "don't give up, there's still more good than bad, more love than hate, more beauty than ugliness". But I wasn't sure I believed it myself.

Instead I told her "let's go to Italy together! I'll get a job, a proper one; I'll give you a baby, whatever you want!"

I told her "I love you".

I told her "don't leave me".

Yael's always known me better than I've known myself.

- "You won't last a year in that life! You'll give me a family, then you'll be miserable. Don't waste yourself, Nico. You are amazing. You are beautiful. The travel, the escaping, the loneliness, you have it in your blood. The running away, it lives deep in you since you were nine. Not me. I have the Jewish blood, Nico. I tried denying it for years, but I've got no strength left to fight it. I've got the blood of the settler. My ancestors searched the earth for hundreds of years looking for a place where to settle, where they could feel safe at last. My land is my fate. But you Nico, you've got the traveler's blood running in your veins. It's your curse, not mine."

She left me there, half dead, quartered in that bed where so many men had laid naked before, hovering a couple of bucks to Candy, or Sugar, or what's-her-face. Yael slid like a panther insider her clothes, grabbed her passport and left for good. I spent another two days laying on those filthy sheets impregnated with her scent. Maybe I was trying to make sense of what had just happened; maybe I was waiting for something to happen. Eventually I had to eat. So I got up. I took to the streets – all of them. I roamed Istanbul like a tourist, taking pictures in my mind. I sat in front of the Bosphorus for hours, counting the boats; letting the hundreds diamonds shining on the Mediterranean waters hypnotize me. When I got tired and realized I was too damn smug to beg for food, I hitchhiked my way back to Italy.

I was determined to prove her wrong. I looked for a proper job, starting with international institutions. But a lot had changed in ten years. I didn't have the diplomas, I had too little documented experience. I tried writing a CV like you're supposed to but I had nothing to put on it. Smuggler? Truck driver? Fighter of the world's silent revolutions? Apparently those were not experiences I could talk about. And not only with employers or recruiters. Soon I realized I couldn't talk about my past with anybody. I had become an outcast. Literally.

So here you go. Here you have it. Why I work for ten bucks an hour in a stupid restaurant. Why I don't write about my life any more than I talk about it. Why I can be neither normal nor extraordinary. Neither the bad one, nor the good one. Why I wake up with whisky in my mouth and a half-burnt cigarette lying on the floor where I let it fall last night. I turn over and there's nobody lying next to me. No pyramidal nose to protect me from the obnoxious light piercing the shades.

I remember her, dancing naked beneath the burgundy ceiling, surrounded with passion red, and her caramel skin glowing in the dim light of the fading summer day. I remember the weight of her body trying to crush mine, every inch of her skin trying to meet mine, her fingers locking my fingers, her entire self combining with mine. I remember the smell of her hair brushing my face as she nested her nose in the curve of my neck. I remember the feeling every time I feared for her life. There was nothing I wouldn't do to protect her.

Every time she got too near to the fire lines. Every time she'd push a soldier a little bit too far. She loved to post herself in the face of danger, but she would never tell me; I was too protective, she'd say. Then my tigress grew tired of roaring in vain.

I want to call her. I shouldn't: I've failed. It's too late for me to be normal. Yet I need to call her. I need to try to convince her after all, not let her go, never let her go. But I don't have her number. But we haven't talked in 13 months and 3 days. Ok, maybe I did count a bit…

She's probably with someone by now: a normal guy, one that wears white shirts and smells of cologne. Not like me with my used T-shirts and my smell of burnt tobacco. She must be with Mister Perfect. I can see him perfectly: shaved, proper, the kind that gives five bucks a month to charity and refuses to buy an I-phone "because it's made by kids in China, you know?" That's what she wanted: a normal life, with a kind normal guy.

I just wish to hear her voice. She'll help me remember that's there are good people out there. She'll give me strength to bounce back and take control of my life. Why can't I do that? Why can't I take control of my own life?

You think I'm pathetic? You might be right. I must look damn pathetic lying in my own uselessness. Maybe it's better if I just turn on the TV instead. Look, here comes Berlusconi recovering from his face-lift number 56. And here comes the empty Plaza del Sol in

Madrid. Where have they gone, all those *Indignados*? Where have they left us? Oh and look, here is Cairo! There are protesting again, there are not happy with the new guys in charge either. We really don't learn from history, do we? I remember a book about the French Revolution Mamma Maria bought me when I was about twelve. She had me read it to her. She wanted to know about the Kings and the Queens; how their head fell, how the poor people won in the end. So I read to her about the guillotine and the sans-culotte. Yet I never read to her the second half of the book: the part where the Kings and Queens are replaced with a tiny emperor described as small, proud, authoritative, and loud. Already back then I could think of so many contemporary rulers who fit the description. It would make me laugh while Mamma Maria had fallen asleep, dreaming of headless princesses. Meanwhile, gone the dreams of the plebs! Salute your new Emperor O puny ones!

That's the way it is my dears! You thought you could change history with your Tweets and your blogs. You didn't see it coming? It's in our genes. It's been there all along. Rome, Genghis Khan, Versailles… an Emperor falls and another rises. We all believed in Obama, we all believed in every one of our revolutions, and I'm supposed to give you more hope? Tommaso, he says we owe to give hope to the youth, he doesn't see hope is a blinding poison. I shall not give hope, they don´t need it. What they need is a force so powerful it pulls them from their chairs and sofas. Like in those Van Damn movies. He´s tied up, he can´t move, he´s tired. But comes the bad guy holding the pretty lady and here rushes in Schwarzy or Bruce or one of them, all fired up, their strength suddenly augmented by that most powerful feeling: rage! Get up, you people! Don´t you feel angry yet? They've taken your money, your land, your pride, your dignity. Don't you feel like striking back? Rage is beautiful. Put one truly angry man in power and you'll see him take over the world!

I turn over to sit up straight, my blood is boiling. Cursed be Yael for knowing me so well. Cursed be my father – he'd be so happy to know I'm no better than he was. Cursed be I, for thinking I could touch the sky - if only my arm were just a bit longer.

Remember the road.

Cherish every moment of it.

Cherish the achievement.

Sit in a room of enemies and learn to cherish them as human, looking at them in the eyes, not at the passport. Challenging views, opening to the overwhelming equality of US. Equals in our hopes as much as in our traumas. Oscillating between statuses – persecutor, victim, occupier, foreigner, stranger.

Then accept to lose it all.

Cherishing the void, the absence of definition.

Letting go of all identities.

And discover that we, still, remain the naked humanity of ourselves.

The security officer looks at my brand new passport and does not even budge. Like a robot, he stamps it and hands it over to me, his eyes running through me completely empty. I'm not even sure he actually looked at me. It seemed more like he was looking through me, at something very far away, like a long-lost memory. I head straight to the door. No checked-in luggage. I'm just a weekend traveler whose life is interesting to no one. Last time I was here, the second Intifada was raging. I went through this airport a clueless young man and was held in custody for hours. You know: a twenty-something Italian kid; I must have been trying to smuggle out some diplomatic documents or some dangerous armaments.

- "Did any Palestinian give you anything at any time?"
- "No."
- "Did you have any kind of relationship with a Palestinian?"
- "I bought them food."
- "Did you have any kind of relationship with a Palestinian woman?"
- "No."
- "Did you engage in dangerous activities while in the Palestinian territories?"

And so on, and so on… But nothing of the kind this time. It's been ten years. Now everything is different. Palestine has achieved statehood now. A state dribbled with settlers and no strength left to fight, but a state at last.

Out in the street everything looks similar yet unrecognizable. Gone all the armed forces everywhere. They have given place to shopping mall and skyscrapers. I get down the bus just outside of Florentin. I want to walk a bit. Remember the place; prepare my words. What if she opens the door? What if she does still live there? What if she's married? What if she slams the door in my face? Maybe I shouldn't have come. I am always so impulsive! What is wrong with me? But what can I do? I have to see her; it is stronger than me.

A lot of things are stronger than me, I discovered.

Her house stands at the corner of Mesilat Wolfson with Hakishon. I station myself just a few blocks away, at the only bar I could find that had survived since the good ol' days. Arik's bar on the corner of Matalon and Hahalutsim is the same place, same owner, same decoration. Yet I can't recognize it. The passionate discussions about politics and human rights have given place to chilled-out guys with a pink or yellow cotton scarf around their neck and a MacBook sitting on their lap. They drink coffee and exchange a smile with the waiter once in a while. It suddenly dawns on me how much of a dis-adapted I am. I really don't seem to fit anywhere anymore. Everybody seems to have moved on, but me. Yael has moved on too, probably. It's quite certain actually. She's a solid down-to-earth woman. She's probably running some NGO in downtown Tel Aviv and I'm here sitting in my brand-less jeans trying to think of a speech.

"Yael, I need you. I'm lost. Take me back!"

Ah! I might as well shoot myself in the foot. I really suck at this.

"Yael. I'm not amazing, I'm not beautiful. You were wrong. I'm just a stranded dog chasing its tail. I don't want to go anywhere anymore. I want to be with you. Be your man!"

Right! What a man! I got no fancy scarf and I got no life, just a miserable waiter's wage, which I burnt away in the flight ticket.

As I am lost in my thoughts, taking pleasure in despising myself, in decorticating every one of my cons, every single piece of me that does not fit in the big puzzle of our ever-changing society, everything that is not cool about me, everything that I have left unsolved through the years of fighting myself – as I sit moving my fingers on the wooden panel attached to the outside window where I have forgotten my long cooled-down coffee, I fail to notice the pair of feet dangling in the air, and the trench coat falling down around the stool, and the mass of curly black hair hiding a woman's face, a woman who is looking straight in front of her, watching me in the mirroring glass of the bar's street window.

Slowly, methodically, the sun goes down, flashing its ray across the woman's face, drawing on my anxious hands the triangular shape of a leaning pyramid. I freeze, unable to take my eyes away from my shaking hands.

- "Yael?"
- "I saw you sitting here. I was walking down Matalon on my way home."
- "You still live in that house?"
- "Yes."
- "I was practicing my speech for you."

I still can't look at her. My eyes are glued to my hands and my hands are nailed to the wood. She doesn't look at me either. She just sits there. Her hands on her knees. Her feet dangling in the void. She's so tiny Yael, yet her shadow is gargantuan. It eats me alive, sucking my flesh and spitting only the bones, my frail bones jingling savagely in the silence between us.

- "Do you want to give it to me now?"
- "No. (silence) I forgot it."

She extends her left hand towards me. Slowly. Unsecure. She seems to shake a bit but I can't say for sure. Then slowly she lays her warm shaky hand on my cold shaky hand and leaves it there to rest. Her warmth gives me just enough courage to turn my head, just enough strength to finally dare look at her. I'm expecting her commiserating gaze to burn my skin. I can feel her pitying me, realizing that the rebellious man that she left has turned into a miserable cockroach. Because of her. All because of her.

As my eyes meet her eyes at last, as I am ready to die on the spot at any sign of pity, I find the most beautiful pair of eyes, green from the dying daylight, moist from the nascent tears. Before I can start breathing again, she extends her arms around me and pulls me to her, furiously embracing me, kissing my neck, leaving my cheeks humid with her tears, blessing my lips with her eyelashes, stealing my heart all over again with her intensity.

- "I missed you, Nico."
- "I missed you too, *bimba*."

Her hand in my hand, her pain, my pain disappearing in the depth of our past, we walk down the avenue that leads to the beach, that very beach where I first met her. She fills in the gaps for me.

- "So it turns out I can't do normal. I can't talk to anybody, I can't find myself in any place. I became friend to the freaks, the outcasts. I can't do normal. I can only do stranded dogs like you. (She laughs.) Every day I go down to the beach to look over the Mediterranean Sea, far away over to Europe. I feel the sand beneath my feet and think about all those people on "the other side". Under my feet the sand, under theirs the dust, under yours the bitumen. I think about all these feet, the naked ones, the tired ones, the high-heeled ones. A few steps away a bunch of twenty-something kids are lounging, sunbathing, enjoying their army leave, deaf to the blasts coming from "the other side". I used to sit right there on that beach just like them. But I never got deaf. I never accepted. I understand now that I have been a dis-adapted since the day I refused to follow the flock. I don't belong here anymore. I don't belong anywhere anymore. Nor here nor there. Nor on this side nor on the other. Turns out I'm just like you after all. And I chased you away. (She cries.) I chased away the only person who truly got me. Will you take me back, Nico? Will you take my stupid heart back?"

I look at my reflection in her eyes, I look at the stranded dog that I am and I feel endlessly happy.

- "I'll take your stupid heart back any time, Yael!"

This is us: nation-less vagabonds stuck in between all lines of discrimination. I am the ungrateful heir of Don Mario's realm, born from corruption and abuse. She is the disobedient daughter of a war general, born from violence and frustration. Forever expats, never sheep. People have given us so many etiquettes. But they never stuck. We are all born barefoot, aren't we? Me, her, that Palestinian kid, that Israeli soldier, my mother, Don Mario. We won't save the world, we won't fix humanity, but we will contribute to building a consciousness without frontiers nor definitions and we will belong everywhere.

And so I win.

I remember the road.

I cherish every moment of it.

I cherish the achievement.

I sat in a room of enemies and learned to cherish them as human, looking at them in the eyes, not at the passport. Challenging views, opening to the overwhelming equality of US. Equals in our hopes as much as in our traumas. Oscillating between statuses – persecutor, victim, occupier, foreigner, stranger, apt, unapt.

I lost it all, then won it back.

And I discovered, after so many miles, that not all the roads lead to Rome.

9- LA NIÑA DEL TAROT

Punta Arena, Chile, 2012

"It's time." I am sitting in the on-call room. The TV is spitting dramas on mute. A fluffy woman is recounting – tears in her puffed-up eyes – looking terrified yet interestingly well arranged for an "impromptu" interview. The subtext runs in red at the bottom of the screen "violent Pit-bull loose in the streets of La Florida spreads panic and terror." How can this be national news, I don't know. I've given up on media long ago. Especially here, where they stage up news info as if a 90s' Mexican sitcom. I turn off the TV – although I'm pretty sure some nurse will come and turn it on again as soon as I'll step out. Outside the door, a bunch of lady doctors are exchanging their respective "hysterical old lady" stories.

- "No te crei lo que me dijo la vieja culia'a! "You gave me the wrong drug, Doctor." La vieja tonta, cachai! Well, at the end I got an intuition and asked her "are you taking the drugs, or somebody else?" – "What does it matter?" she answered, pero tu cachai la hueona? Well, turned out she was feeding it to her husband, a freaking drug for menopause!"

- "Nooooo, hueona! 'Ta picada la vieja!"

Stories like that have been a part of my daily life for the past seven years. During my intern years in La Concepcion, over the years of training in Antofagasta, Calama, Curico, and all over the north of Chile. I recently turned a Resident. A comfy position as a trauma doctor in Punta Arena: Patagonia, la Terra de Fuego, the end of the world. I love it here. Calm and silence. As I am walking down the hallway I recall my whole life. Dead man's flashback: my whole life condensed in those five minutes it takes me to walk from the on-call room to my boss' office. How did nothing ever happen to me? How am I here, alive, in one piece? I have seen so many people torn apart, separated from their legs, interiors out, knifes planted straight in their chest, head smashed flat by some mining machine. Especially in the North. Over there you see all kind of casualties. Men half flattened down by those giant vehicles. Most of the time it's their fault. Most of the time they just didn't pay attention, or they just "believed that". Stupid people. So many of them. But they are good people, most of them. Often they tell me their stories, how they met their wives, how they are planning on buying them some nice jewelry one day. Sometimes they are out there, in the desert, for weeks without coming back home. Days after days of rocks and sand. Days and days of living a tiny ant life. Tiny ants maneuvering such giant trucks. Digging trucks, flattening trucks, carrier trucks.

Down here in the extreme South you don't see much trauma. Mostly I get half-frozen tourists. They want to explore the Terra de Fuego and they come back with a couple toes missing. Besides that, life here is a quiet routine of cut fingers and broken legs. It's funny when you think everything I've seen, everything people around me have gone through. Young men gone missing, old communists shot in the back, miners smooched flat, thousands of people horrifyingly wounded. I never got as much as a finger broken. I've never been sick, never struggled to find a job. I'm 32 and kicking like a young man. Maybe because life threw all the bad at me by the time I celebrated my twelfth birthday. Maybe we each get a certain amount of hardship. Some get it bit by bit throughout their lives. Others, like me, get it all at once at a very early age. And then that's it: all the bad is over.

So what have I been doing with all that good luck? When was the last time I took a vacation, a risk, a challenge? When was the last time I let myself feel, really feel?

There was this girl from Mexico. I was on my afternoon break. I was sitting in my usual spot against the wall at the very same coffee place where I go every day, at 5pm sharp. Every afternoon I go to Aukargërü and have a cup of tea with a *dobladita* bread with ham and cheese. I like routine. I have changed home so many times in my life; as a child I would move from one area of Santiago to the other every six months or so. As an adult I moved from city to village, from the deserts of the North to the glaciers of the South. The more I travelled, the more I yearned for rituals, immutable places, familiar faces.

Aukargërü is my familiar face. He doesn't talk much. Sometimes he mumbles poems in Mapu-dungun. Sometimes I think he is blessing my food; sometimes cursing it. There aren't many Mapuche left in Punta Arena, but those who stay are strong and quiet like ancient trees. I read once that Aukargërü means *Free Fox*. I wish I had a cool name like him. Free Fox… I wonder what would be my Mapuche name. *Lonely Healer From The Big City*?

Hers would be *Black Panther*. When she entered the place she gazed around like a black panther, she fluidly slipped through the room and sat at the widest table in the place. She took off a tiny velvet purse and undid the tie gracefully. My *dobladita* was hanging in the air, half-way between the table and my mouth, still waiting for me to take a bite at it. But I had forgotten. I was in a theatre and the lights were set on her. She ordered a coffee and started spreading Tarot cards all around the table. The waitress, a disgraceful woman with high cheekbones and caramel skin, indelicately left the cup of steaming coffee in front of her, uncaring of the cards occupying the stage. The panther went on moving around her cards, reflecting for a while on one, or the other. She'd make funny grins each time she'd take a sip of her coffee. She waived eerily at Aukargërü, planted behind the counter, moaning unintelligible words over a cup of tea. He was sweating heavily despite the chilly temperature, sporting a sleeveless tank-top while I myself was wrapped inside two pullovers and a woolen coat. Aukargërü moved slowly among the tables, putting all his weight on one foot, then the other, left, right, waddling over to the dark sibyl.

- "Do you have *real* coffee?"

The Patagonian bear gauged the meaning of the question for a while, probably thinking of a funny reply to what he assumed must have been her way of joking. Yet the frown on her face must have stopped him because instead he cleared his throat, shifted his weight over to his right foot, and wiped his hands against his jeans.

- "No m'am, we don't have no *real* coffee. We only have fake coffee. But if you want I do have real bread that my woman she made it herself, and I do have real cheese that my brother he makes it from his own cows, and I have real ham that we make it in my family from our pigs; but we don't have no real coffee and we don't have no real fruit juice either. We m'am live of what we have, of what our land has to offer us."

She drowned into her cards, blushing like a little girl. She mumbled a *"lo siento"* and started muddling her cards frenetically. The bear waddled away, satisfied, and I felt bad for her. In my sweetest voice I hailed her from my table.

- "Don't worry, miss, you haven't done anything wrong. He's just a grumpy old man. People are like that here. Tough. But they are good people you know, very good people. The cold and the wind shield them – that's all."
- "I know, it's ok, it's my fault. He must think I'm *quika*!"
- "Ha-ha-ha! That word sounds very cute in your mouth. I see you're learning Chilean already! But don't worry; I don't think you're snob. Just a little bit out of your comfort zone, maybe…"
- "Maybe… Do you want me to read you the Tarot?"
- "Oh, I don't know… I don't really believe in that stuff."
- "That's okay. Just for fun!"

She made me pick three cards, then two more. She turned them over, one after the other, revealing artistic figures. A four of cups, upright. The wheel of fortune, upright. The hermit, dignified. A three of wands, reversed. Death, upright.

She looked at me intensely, with a mix of tenderness and compassion.

- "What?"

- "I see that you are very successful professionally. Still, I can sense clearly that the trail of your life has been sowed with loss and grief. Something very tormented lays in you that has been pacified with quiet resolution. See the Hermit? It's right next to the Wheel of Fortune, but tilted. He doesn´t want to look at her. You are turning away from potentially great happiness. You picked Death, but it appears as a companion in your life. Not a threat. You don't fear it, you welcome it like an old friend. The Four of Cups is showing you a new path, but you'll have to decide whether you want to take it or not."

- "Do you see love?"

She laughed silently, with her mouth wide opened. I don't even know why I asked her that. I'm not one to worry about love. But it came to my mind and I burped it out like a child. She got serious again and dramatically scanned the table with her dark pupils, like a little girl absorbed in her art work.

- "Well… the reversed Three of Wands speaks of unrealized dreams and the Four of Cups talks about a need for stimulation. Maybe thoughts about family. The presence of the Wheel of Fortune is a good sign. If you want love, you'll get it, but you'll have to fight that Three of Wands. It is holding you back. Something in your past prevents you from letting anybody in. An abandon maybe… You need to fight that Three of Wands. Move past your traumas… Get back to living."

She raised her eyes to look straight at me. Almond-shaped eyes. Deep inside those pupils were burning fires, a strong light coming from inside her. I felt my body waking up, I felt my flesh getting warmed by that intense fire, and I felt my stomach torn with anger. How could she see so much of me in those stupid cards? How dared she revive my past and depict me like a traumatized scared little man?

I wanted to tell her I'm not a coward, I wanted to slap her for belittling me. I wanted to get up and leave the room at once. I thought so many things in that very moment, but not one of those things coincided with what actually followed. Instead of slapping her, instead of getting up and leave, my body leaned forward, forward, forward, till my nose touched her nose and my lips stole a kiss from her. Her cat eyes narrowed, shooting straight into mine. A stream of electricity ran through my body, allowing me to regain consciousness, return to my skin, find the commands to my own body and order it to get up and run. Panicked and ashamed, I disappeared in a whim, my *dobladita* still untouched in its plate.

I reached the door to my boss' office. I knock two times and, without waiting, walk into the office, my speech ready and rehearsed. My boss quickly stashes away a cigarette – always his last one, "I swear!" – and invites me to take a seat.

- "I prefer to stand, if you don't mind."
- "Very well. What's bringing you here, Dr. Araya?"
- "Boss. I need to ask you for a leave. I'm not sure how long. Maybe a month, maybe more."

He frowns with worry.

- "Dr. Araya! This is so sudden. What happened? Aren't you happy here?"
- "I am happy, but I need to figure some things out. It's time I give my life a new purpose."
- "What will you do?"
- "I can't tell for sure yet. I'll figure it out along the way, I guess."
- "Dr. Araya, I hope you know what you're doing! Of course I can't say no to you, you're a free man, but you'll be missed. I hope you keep me informed, and let me know if you ever need anything."
- "I will, boss."
- "Whatever it is that you're going after, I wish you luck, son."
- "Thanks Sir, but I'll be just fine."

Two pair of jeans. Four pair of socks. Four boxers. Three t-shirts and a pullover. Trekking shoes. Flip-flops. A toothbrush. Sunglasses. A book about Tarot. A one-way ticket to Calama.

"Tea or coffee?" The stewardess bends over my neighbor to hand me my cup of coffee. It's not real coffee, but I don't know the difference. Actually, I don't think I ever had real coffee. I wonder what it tastes like.

"We are starting our descent towards the city of Calama. Please return to your seat and attach your seatbelt. We will arrive in Calama at 8:55am. Temperature on land is 25°C. Windy. The captain of this flight wishes you a nice stay. Together with the crew, we thank you for choosing LAN airlines today."

Dust, dogs and fleas. Calama has not changed a bit. As ugly as always. It's not past 10am and the sun is already burning on my back. I am grateful for the desert sun has no pity for me. I climb up the bus to San Pedro de Atacama. The seats are wild and comfortable. I fall asleep as soon as I sit down, not waking up until the double-decked bus reaches my final destination.

The sun is blinding. The low mud houses do not provide any shadow; they leave me exposed to the harshness of nature. I walk randomly from one street to the other, letting the memories rush back from the last time I was here, ten years back. I had just graduated, 1st of my class. The youngest too. I still had another five years of specialization and internships to go through, and I had just recently managed to find closure with my past. Manuel's letter had drowned into the depths of the ocean and my mum was returning the kind smile of our neighbor, finally opening up to another man for the first time in twelve years.

I came to San Pedro de Atacama with a bunch of fellow graduates. We spent five days drinking and partying in the desert. Those were the days before I sew up bodies cut in half or spent hours patching people burnt to the point that they did not look human anymore. Partying till dawn has not really been part of my scenario since then. The last Pisco, I drank it on February 27, 2010. I was completing my residency in Santiago's public hospital San Juan de Dios. I had a night off so I had gone out for beers with old friends. The beers soon turned into Pisco, and the Pisco into more Pisco. Early before dawn, the earth shook stronger than I had ever experienced. I was trying to find my way from the bar to my apartment but fell at every other step. The blood rushed to my brain, giving me the impression of soberness. Yet I could not stand, I could not walk, I was being rocked like a baby by the earth itself. I swayed from left to right and right to left while my phone kept beeping 131 furiously, calling me in to receive the hundreds of surgical traumas that would most likely follow. I came in an hour later, unshaved, un-showered, looking just like somebody who had been catapulted over to a war zone. In the clinic, fractured legs, minor head injuries, and a few concussions were coming in the door in a continuous flow, but no dead people, no horrendous smashed-down skulls, nothing to the extent of what I had expected, considering the intensity of the earthquake. Yet, at the little hours of the morning, an old lady came in. Shaking, pointing at the cab parked outside. She was frail, so frail. We got her husband out of the car, carried it inside while the wife stood in the middle of the corridor, lost, in shock, her eyes covered in a hazy veil. We couldn't save her husband. He had suffered a heart attack and at his old age, there's no coming back. I never forgot her; her curved down figure sitting in the hall, incapable to decide what to do next. She stayed there all night, looking at her lifeless hands folded in her laps. She'd refuse to leave. She'd refuse to sleep. I sat next to her for a good while, trying to somehow absorb her pain. I concentrated on the energy she was exhaling and tried to create a flow, letting her dolor rest inside me. I could take it, I thought. I was strong enough. I got home exhausted, feeling immensely sad, carrying around, in the shadow of my steps, the grieving pain of an old lady whom I was never to see ever again.

I haven't touched alcohol since.

When I travelled to San Pedro, ten years ago, that was the furthest from Santiago anyone in my family had ever been. At the time there weren't that many buses driving up, and the picturesque village was not that hippy-chic hub I'm discovering today. Yesterday the streets were nothing but a mud path streaked by the clogs of the donkeys and the paws of the street dogs. Today those streets are crowded with European and Argentinian backpackers. They all wear the same baggy trousers in a declination of colors from dust to sand. They exhibit colored scarfs bought from the local artisanal market, and they go up and down the Caracoles Street like dromedaries' packs, bending under the weight of their super-equipped backpacks, searching for the cheapest hostel. In between that crowd of wannabe-travelers, I discover myself an odd misfit. Outside a hostel, a man is smoking weed, disinhibited, following with half an eye the pretty blond girls in their Indiana Jones costumes.

- "Good afternoon Sir. Would you have a room for me?"

He smiles warmly at me, revealing yellow teeth bigger than his entire face.

- "I got a bed in a room with five other girls."

He's got a French accent that you couldn't cut with a Swiss knife.

- "Mmm. Don't you have a single room?"

Now he stares at me like I just said the most ridiculous thing he's ever heard.

- "Really? You don't want to share the room with five girls from the States? *Quel sot*! They are on Spring Break... young, hot and stupid. You don't look too bad. You'd have a shot, you know? I already got dibs on the little blond one, but the others are all yours!"

I mess with the idea in my mind, I can't say I don't, but the days when I woke up hangovered next to a girl whose name I could not remember are long gone.

- "Thanks for the offer, man, but I'll rather have a single room."
- "All right, all right. You, Sir, don't know how to live, huh? Gotta chill! You're in San Pedro!"
- "Yes indeed. Yes, indeed."

I leave my bag on the bed that shrieks under the weight. The room is cramped, only illuminated with the last rays of light piercing through the shutters. I walk to the bathroom, freshen up with freezing water. The mirror throws back at me an image that I recognize way too well. I'm a properly shaved man in a town invaded by bearded man from the caverns' age. I'm a guy with a recent haircut in a place where the last barber must have gone bankrupt thirty years ago. I'm a top-class trauma surgeon in a land where marijuana is the most advanced medicine they've ever seen. Still, despise all the oddness that pours from me, the memory of those burning cat eyes upon me is reassuring: I'm exactly where I need to be.

I rush my hand through my hair, trying to untidy it, pulling it up with my fingers. I flush water on my face and brush my teeth, then grin at the mirror once more. "Come on handsome! You can do this."

I open the bathroom door to a room already dipped into the ink of the night. Outside, in the courtyard, the French guy is lighting up a fire while a seemingly Brazilian Adonis is playing *Stairway to Heaven*. With his long perfectly knitted dreads and his dark golden skin, he is a walking stereotype. Sitting on huge plane tree logs, the five American girls are living up to the description: blond, delightfully promiscuous… scrumptious is the word that first comes to my mind. Their laughs resonate against the burnt sienna mud walls. The host is exhibiting his smoke-tainted teeth to the blondest of the girls, serenating her with the promise of a later rave party in the Moon

Valley. Ten years ago I practiced sand-board in that valley. Sand board on the Moon. What a feeling!

If only I had known back then what was buried right beneath my feet. I have an old score to settle with the desert.

I wake up late. When you're a surgeon, the word late takes another significance. It's late. You're late. It's too late. When you're surgeon, every second counts. Late is not acceptable. Too late means death. You train to feel the time. You learn to think in seconds, while minutes and hours lose all meaning. You don't count the nine hours that you will be spending in the operating room, on your feet, without a minute of rest, but you count the seconds between one beat and the other, between one movement of the scalpel and the other.

I see the clock of my watch marking 8:44am and jump out of bed, searching for my scrubs (I always leave my scrubs neatly folded on the chair right next to my bed, with my white sneakers perfectly clean right underneath). But there are no scrubs, just a small empty bedside table. I lay there for a bit, watching – without seeing it – the white ceiling over my head. I watch a panther dancing against the screen and I see baby panthers, loads of them. Some black, some white. "It's late. Too late." Is it too late for me to believe in fatherhood? Unconsciously I had blocked out the possibility of ever becoming a father. What if I were a bad father? What if I disappeared, what if I couldn't face the responsibility?

My father disappeared in 1991. At that time everything had supposedly gone back to normal. The government was telling us that we were in a democracy and that we had nothing to fear anymore. Peace and freedom had been restored! So eventually my mother and I got convinced. Two years earlier and we would not have doubted a second that he had been abducted by the army. Two years earlier and my mother would have spent her life searching for its rests in the vacuity of the desert, like all these other women who could never forget. But we let the politicians convince us that it could not be. He must have fled, he must have gotten scared and have abandoned us; that was the only explanation. So I got scared too. Scared that I could replicate the pattern, and I ran from all sorts of social commitments. I had girlfriends, sure, but I would always vanish the moment they'd ask for more. I never caressed the idea of matrimony, and even less that of fatherhood. Today, though, everything is different. Today I see Luisa and I see her almond eyes replicated in a multitude of small versions of her. Today paves the way to a multitude of new roads of unknown destinations.

I know she's supposed to arrive today. Hostel people are chatty in Punta Arena. They confessed everything about her in exchange for a free consult.

- "Oh, you're looking for that pretty Mexican girl, ain't you? Sweet girl. Luisa… yep, that's right, Luisa Ramirez or something like that. A little bit crazy I think. She kept offering to read the Tarot for me. Like I believe that magic bullshit. So whatcha wanna know? Where she went? Well I don't know where she went now, but I can tell you she's planning on getting to San Pedro de Atacama in a couple weeks. She's travelling through Chile. Like a hippie! Where in San Pedro? Ah well, you see, I've got a cousin there. People in the north are so lazy! They don't do nothing all day, you know. So my cousin he said, "Pacita, I tell you, I'm gonna work in the north, enjoy the warmth, and get rich!" Ahahah! Poor fool. But truth is, he ain't doing badly. He opened a hostel there, in San Pedro. I hear he ain't getting rich, but he sure is enjoying himself alright! So, anyway, I told your girl to stay with him at the hostel. He's a good guy, he'll treat her well. The name? Ah right. Hostal Elim it's called. Elim is my cousin. The man's always been a little bit conceited. He likes to have his name written in tall letters. Ahahahaha!"

She went on laughing as I walked away, already plotting a plan in my head.

I don't go to her hostel. Instead I look for the best coffee shop in town, the one that makes *real* coffee, like she said.

I want to let her find me.

I sit down at the table against the wall, the one that has the best sight to the door. I order a piece of quiche – something fancy to inaugurate my new-found unpredictability – and a coffee, a real one. Then, I take out the book about Tarot I bought a few days earlier. I'll wait for her here. She'll come. I know she'll come. She'll see me and she'll sit at my table. She'll look surprise and I'll pretend to be as well. "You? Here? What a surprise!" She'll smile, she'll know I'm acting but she won't get angry. Quite the opposite, she'll feel flattered. Maybe she'll even play the game.

- "Actually, I knew I'd find you here", I'd say.
- "Oh really? How did you know?"
- "The cards told me."
- "And the cards don't lie?"
- "Only humans lie."
- "Do you lie?"
- "Never!"
- "So you'll tell me why you escaped that day?"
- "I didn't escape, 'tis your beauty that blew me away."

She'd blush and let her hand flutter behind her ear to arrange a lock of her midnight hair, which will immediately fall back over. With the movement, the light will draw streaks of fire on her hair, the flame of her ebony fur gliding against the sizzling gold of her skin.

The waitress brings in the coffee. She winks at me and chirps in a delightful Argentinian accent "Espresso para Vos!" and exposes the minuscule cup in front of me, turning it slightly to place the handle in the right angle. The black liquid paints curves of creamy foam, shivering under my pulse. I look around me. I like the place. It bears traces of its visitors. A picture, a travel book, a perfume. The coffee machine exhales fumes of the beans being crushed, serving the only purpose of my delight. It's an awakening of my senses, an education of my palate. The time has slowed down. Everything is taking its place. She'll come. I know she'll come. I take off my watch and call in the waiter.

- "You like watches?"
- "Che, yeah. I don't mind them."
- "Here's for you."
- "Huh?"
- "Please take it."
- "Sir! I couldn't!"
- "Yes, you could."

She walks away dumbfounded and amused, already wriggling the watch into the pocket of her pinafore. I finally breathe, liberated from the obsessional need to check my wrist every minute. She'll come. I know she'll come. Time has turned insignificant.

I sniff the two drops of black liquid like a dog sniffs a piece of meat handed to him by a stranger. I bring the cup to my lips, taking a quick sip, like those old ladies sipping on their tea in last century's British movies. The coffee drips slowly like a river of liquid chocolate. It is bitter, creamy; a touch of tobacco hits my nostrils.

The smell brings back slices of my life carefully tucked away in unused parts of my brain. November 5, 2007. I was in Santiago, visiting after six months of training in Iquique. Six months trapped in between the vast Pacific Ocean and the deathly Atacama Desert. I'd been in Santiago five hours and I'm already missing the silence, the sweet comfort of the heat, the sun sizzling all things from above, and the ocean fizzing with the light, roaring with the winds, inhospitable yet so tempting; it's violent turquoise endlessness contrasting with the calm warmness of the burnt-sienna desert taking over the horizons, infinitely. And right in the middle of that monstrous fight between water and land, between one infinite and the other, an idle strip of life, a few thousand houses, some palm trees, and an army of tiny white boats. Back in Santiago everything smelled of smog and gasoline.

Mum called. She said I've got to come. It's important. In the barrio Lastarria where I met her, coffee shops had started mushrooming everywhere. They served coffee in little cups and cakes in big plates. They hosted elegant girls sitting at their table, reading a book, smoking a cigarette, laughing silently with their hands covering their mouths. They had menus with names I had never heard before:

cappuccino, mokaccino, ristretto. As I waited for my mum, I stood there, watching the girls crossing their soft legs, flashing their hair, hiding their little white teeth. I remember the smell of coffee titillating my nostrils. Bitter, violent, peppery. My mum came alone, a pink shawl draped around her shoulders. Her greying hair were cut short, the paleness of her face was accentuated by the intensity of her carmine lipstick.

- "Should we sit there, at the terrace?"
- "No. Too fancy. Let's got sit in the parc, *hijo*. Let's go sit in the park like in the old days."

She spread her shawl on the grass and carefully sat on it. She's so tiny my mum, but so strong. Her pain-molded strength irradiated from her, intimidating. I didn't know if I should have hugged her or let her embrace me. Who protected the other? Who carried the other's hopes?

- "They found his body."

She looked straight at me, waiting for a reaction, but I was suspended in time.

- "They found his body out there in the Atacama desert, deep below the rocks."

She kept silent for a few seconds, giving me an opportunity to talk but I gathered nothing to say.

- "A woman found him. One of those women who keep searching for their husbands, their sons, their disappeared relative. She found bones. Human bones. She must have prayed so hard that it may be her beloved. Years searching the desert to finally found another woman's husband. She never stopped remembering, and I never stopped trying to forget. Fate is random, *hijo*."

She did not stop watching me, the whole time – her pupils burning.

- "They analyzed the bones, from the teeth they could determine the identity. They called me. They said they had found him. They were running exams to determine the cause of death. They said they'd call back. I stayed by the phone. I did not move. I did not sleep. I did not think a thing. I just waited. The next day they called back. He was killed. One gunshot in the head. Violent death. Probably didn't suffer long. They asked me what to do with the body. Did I want a burial or cremation?"

- "…"

- "The cremation is tomorrow."

- "…"

- "I got you a black shirt. I know you don't have any black shirt. So I got you one. And black trousers too. But you're so thin. Maybe they won't fit. You're so thin. Just like Manuel when he was your age. Just like Manuel."

Her big dark eyes filled up with tears, which she immediately erased. She is not a woman to cry in public.

The remnants of coffee draw figures at the bottom of my cup as I rock it softly back and forth. Somebody comes through the door. I peak, hoping it's her. Enters a tall guy with a blond beard and long golden hair. Where is she?

I don't mind the wait. I used to sit by my patients for hours, waiting on them to wake up after a surgery, unaware of the passing of the hours. And how many years did I wait for my father to return? Sure I eventually gave up on him, but not at first. At first I did believe something had happened. Maybe he had been abducted, maybe he was being tortured, maybe he was working on some very confidential mission. I extrapolated every scenario a young boy's imagination allows. Till I threw his letter in the ocean. That's the day I stopped waiting for him.

In life you've got to make mistakes. As many as you can. You've got to fall in every hole and trip on every bump; and trust blindly to get a chance to be coldly betrayed, stabbed in the back like a dog. You've got to open the doors to your house without fear, so that they can rob it all from you, leave you naked and alone.

When I was ten years old, as I watched my father leave to never return, I tasted disgust in my guts, I felt my stomach turn sour, acid reflux burning up my throat. When I was twelve I punched the wall a few inches right of my mother's head after she told me she was done waiting for him. When I was fifteen I woke up in the gutters, alone, at seven in the morning, a young girl poking my arm with a stick.

They had just declared my father a terrorist on the run. I got hammered.

I have hated him. I was so convinced that he must have been alive, somewhere. He must have left with some other woman, must have got scared and fled to another country. He must have been living the life, over there in Europe. They were so many who fled to France, to Germany. He must have been saying *dankeschön* and *guten morgen* to round women with feathers on their felt hat. I threw away his letter, burnt his memory, erased him with all my heart: he couldn't be dead. Despite it all, despite what it would have meant, I always prayed he wasn't dead. My father may have been a coward and a traitor, but at least he was alive somewhere. Somewhere.

It took me over ten years to finally give up on him; to finally convince myself that he would not return. I threw his letter away, I got rid of everything that reminding me of him. I threw my memories away, or so I thought. The recovery of his body opened the dungeons of my memory, only to find them more alive and hurtful than ever. My father wasn't a coward, nor a traitor. He did not abandon us. My father was killed. We might not ever know why or how, but that doesn't matter. The weight that has been lifted from my mother's shoulder is the weight of sixteen years of sorrow and doubt. Sixteen years without knowing whether to mourn or despise, whether to feel loss or rage.

The day I went to the morgue with my mother to see my father's rests, I did not cry. I looked at those few rescued bones, yellowed by the years, and it downed on me: all these years I had fought so hard to become a surgeon, even when all told me there was no way I'd make it. I was poor, I came from public education… I was a nobody. I had nothing but my rage and conviction and, eventually, over sweat and tears of frustration, I did it. I always thought medicine was my calling. That day I realized it was my curse. Like the Danaides were condemned to perpetually fill perforated jars, I had condemned myself to endlessly save the lives of mortals inevitably destined to die, paying back to the universe the one life I could not ever save.

The waitress comes back.

- "How was the coffee, Sir?"
- "Delicious! I could come back here every day just to enjoy the coffee!"
- "Oh, well, I hope the new owner won't change the coffee then!"
- "The new owner?"
- "Yeah, the current owner is ill. Cancer. He can't keep up with the place anymore. So he's looking to sell."
- "Oh. I'm sorry about that. Any offers yet?"
- "Yeah, a couple, but they all want to change the place. They want to transform it into some fancy lounge or something like that. San Pedro is the new hub, they say."
- "And you don't like the idea?"
- "Of course not! Look at this place. Everything here is the result of Roberto's passion. Roberto is the owner. The tiles on the walls: Roberto made a trip to Andalusia twenty years ago. He loved the place so much that he asked a friend to make those tiles especially for him so that every day he'd feel a little bit as if he

were in Sevilla. And that painting: a present from a regular who used to come here every morning to get his coffee. He died last year of old age, but Roberto says his spirit still comes every morning for his cup of coffee. Roberto prepares it just the same, and leaves it on the corner table, certain that his friend is there, reading his favorite book and sipping on his cup. The idea that tomorrow everything will be wiped out, everything that Roberto has created over the years… no, I don't like it a bit."

- "I understand. You really can feel the history of the place. If I bought it, I wouldn't change a thing!"

She nods with sadness.

- "Well, at least I can make a contribution with another cup of coffee."

Her face lights up and she smiles vividly:

- "Che, right away, Sir!"
- "Juan. My name is Juan."
- "And I'm Eugenia, at your service!"

She winks at me and hops away, joyful again, into the kitchen.

I feel just like this place. A place full of memories owned by a sick man, exposed to the eyes of the passerby. I thought I kept them buried deep, invisible to the others, a box of unused souvenirs kept away in the cellar of an old mansion. Luisa opened the Pandora box, like a child who secretly climbs up to the mysterious cellar and comes back with his arms full of forgotten broken toys and yellowed pictures of another era. Now all the images are coming back, every smell, every sound is the key to a new nostalgic scavenging.

I wish I could sell my memories like one sells a coffee shop. Give it away for somebody else to redecorate it, make anything they want out of it. They can throw away the memories of my 10th birthday, the image of my mother sitting at the unique table of the house, peeling all the onions she could afford in order to hide her tears. We ate a lot of onions that year. Partly to hide her sorrow, mostly because we could not afford anything else. We had fallen so deep into poverty, without a father and without a cause, but my mother still managed to put a few pesos together to buy my favorite food, special treat for my birthday. There was a tube of pork pâté, and half a tube of cream cheese. I remember I spread half the tube of pâté all at once on my bread slice. I was so excited, and I feared it might all disappear if I as much as blinked.

I wish I could sell those memories, give them away for somebody else to care for them. But what would anybody do of my story? My story has no action, no romance, not even a good hero. I wish I had a good epic to tell and someone to listen.

Right at this moment, a coarse tongue runs through my naked right foot, taking me by surprise and causing me to jump a good inch over my chair. The puppy looks at me with happy eyes, his tail wiggling from side to side. "Here! Here! I'm listening!" he seems to be pleading. He's got the most wonderful silver fur, with shiny black ears pointing up and a large tongue hanging down, curved up at the tip as he goes "hh-hh-hh".

I pat him on the head and scratch him on the back of his neck, then down his back. He lays his head on my knee and barks once: "come on, tell me a story!" I'm hearing in his eyes.

- "You want a story, *perrito*? Alright alright… Once upon a time lived a pretty princess named Luisa. Her skin was color of caramel and her eyes were shaped like almonds. She came from a far far away country, a magic place where bones were so big that a dog had enough to gnaw on for its entire life."
- "Wof!"
- "Ah! Ah! I knew you'd like it! I wish I were a dog like you, free of troubles and chains. Do you think dogs can go along with panthers? Or would they just be left scarred with bites and scratches?"

I look around, stroking the puppy's head as it falls asleep in my lap. I do feel very comfortable here. I feel home. I'm falling in love with the smells of coffee and the fancy quiches, so much I just want to take on writing about all this. Maybe now I do have something interesting to write about. Something profound like Luis Sepúlveda's portraits of the South or something very moving, like Neruda's poems. If only I had that sort of talent to describe things, make people laugh and cry with nothing but my words. Luisa makes me laugh and cry. She breathes life into my body, into my entire world. Even her absence is exciting and inspiring. If she were to tell me that she created this world, painted those dunes and crafted those rocks, I would believe her with unbreakable faith.

-    "Sir, we're closing. I'm sorry."

I step away from my trance. She'll come tomorrow. I know she will.

This is my third day at the coffee shop. I spend the whole day there. She could come in at any time. Eugenia entertains me with stories of her travels, the ones she's done, the ones she dreams about. Eugenia is grounded, joyful, rough a bit, volatile a lot. Sometimes she's cute. Sometimes she's beautiful. She's never twice the same.

She likes to chat with me when there's no one else in the place.

- "You've ever been to Argentina?"
- "No."
- "I'm from Cordoba. Not from Buenos Aires, huh! The Porteños, they're so full of themselves. I know because Chileans tell me all the time! We don't like them much in Cordoba either. I don't know about the people but I've been to Buenos Aires and I loved it! They say it's like being in Italy. Ah! Italy! I wish I could go to Italy. Roma. Venetia. Verona… It must be amazing. Romance! You can roam about the streets in a little white dress, you can sit on the doorsteps of a roman church and boom! Here comes this beautiful Italian man, elegant, charming, and he comes, takes your hand and sweeps you away, teaching you it all about love and romance. It must be wonderful. Not like the men from my valley. Nothing refined there. I mean they're kind and honest, but where's the passion? I never found anyone there who could carry me away and make me feel like a Fellini *heroina*. See, I grew up among horses, taking the tourists out in the valley and showing them the stars. I'd invent constellations. The tourists never budged. Why are tourists so dumb, huh? Always

carrying around their little banana pack, trotting about in their white sneakers, white socks and blue jean shorts. When I travel the world – I want to go around the world, see – when I do I won't even take a camera. I'll just live, experience, record everything in my own mind. Cameras are for tourists to come back home and boast about their holidays. *And this is me with a monkey. And there it's me talking to a local.* Fools!"

She makes me laugh, Eugenia. She makes me forget for a moment that Luisa still hasn't come. But she'll come. Right?

- "So… which countries have you visited?"
- "None."
- "What? You've never been abroad?"
- "Nope"
- "Wow. That's crazy! Don't you miss it?"
- "Why would I? I've never left Chile and yet I've climbed the highest mountains and gazed into the mouths of volcanos. I've gone horseback-riding in native woods and ate fish cooked in the ground under man-made fire. I've crossed the world's most arid desert, trekked through mountains of ice in the Tierra de Fuego and sunbathed at 6000 meters above the ground in the hot springs of the Andes. I've seen the ocean take over the lands, crushing houses under its weight, and I felt the earth shake to its root till I thought it might tear open."

- "Chile is amazing. I can't believe you did all that! But what about the people? Don't you miss discovering other cultures, other perspectives?"

- "People? I don't care much for people, Eugenia. I prefer dogs. I've known all sorts of dogs and they never hurt me the way people did."

Despite her debilitating illness, Roberto has taken an interest in me. On the fourth day, he comes and sits at my table with a game of backgammon.

- "You know how to play?"
- "No."
- "I'll teach you."

He is a tough man, used to giving orders. He frowns every time I make a move that he doesn't judge clever. Eugenia brings him an espresso which he gulps down in one shot without taking his gaze away from the board.

- "So you're waiting on a girl, huh?"

I blush. I'm a 32 year-old man who blushes.

- "Yes."
- "How do you know she'll come here?"
- "The coffee. She likes *real* coffee."
- "Ah! A keeper then!"

I can't tell if he's being sarcastic or spontaneous. His eyes are still glued on the board, shifting from one checker to the other.

- "Is she in love with you?"
- "I don't know. I've only met her once for ten minutes."

Now he looks away from the board and nails his eyes into mine.

- "Are you insane?"
- "Maybe. Or maybe this is only the first step on the road to recovery."
- "Recovery from what?"
- "From the past."
- "That ain't much wise, young man. The past is everything. A man with no past is a very sad man."
- "I treated once a patient with long-term amnesia. He held no memories of his past. Like in the movies. He could not even remember his name. Then one day, for no reason at all, his memory came back. He remembered he'd been tortured as a young man in the early years of the dictatorship. He remembered his wife had cheated on him and abandoned him while he was working as a miner in Chuquicamata. He remembered he'd lost millions of pesos in a trial against his boss who'd fired him after he'd lost half a hand in the trenches. And he remembered he had lost his memory after they assaulted him in the park where he had been sleeping for the past few months, a bottle of cheap whisky for only companion. A couple days after he recovered his memory, he threw himself from his 21st-floor hospital bedroom window."

Roberto stares at me, silent, then looks back down at the board, moves a few white pieces around and declares in a flat voice:

- "I win."
- "And I lose."

Roberto shoots me down with his stare:

- "You gotta get rid of that attitude, young lad. You ain't going far with that mindset."

I feel scolded like a child. That's what my mother said too. "You've got to move on", she said. "You've got to find yourself a nice girl and learn to trust again. Your father did not abandon us, *hijo*. He loved us. And you will love too. And you will be an excellent father."

Mothers can see right through your most shameful fears. When I think of Luisa, my fears fade away, irrelevant caprices of a lonely child. Luisa would be an excellent mother, if only she'd come.

Throughout the days Roberto and I develop what could be called a friendship for two lone wolves like us. He tells me the stories behind every piece in the place. The lamp from his grandma. The Atacamenian statue crafted by his dad who was an artisan. The tacky golden Chinese cat with his hypnotic arm going back and forth, left as a gift by a German couple he'd helped out during a mis-planned trip in the desert. That china pot in the left corner: a haunted left-over of a British general who oversaw the nitrate mine of Santa Elena. It is said that hundreds died under his command, overworked, burnt alive by the desert sun. My father sure had company down under in the desert's soil.

On the other corner, defying it, a white marble statue of two lovers embraced, their lips nearly touching, their naked bodies melting into each other's. That one is a gift from Roberto to his late wife. He had bought it on their wedding day, to symbolize his timeless commitment to her. She had freckles and a mole on the right cheek a bit below the eye. She did not like it. He loved it. She wore a hat, always the same, it was her favorite. She was like that. Only one hat, only one man, her whole life. Yet she'd always say "that one's my favorite". She died at the age of sixty-eight, taken away by an aneurism. She died like that, on the spot, without pain, without words. He still feels her body against his. He still talks to her at night, in the intimacy of their bedroom.

On the tenth day, on my way to Roberto's, I find a puppy. Curled up, little silver furry thing shivering with the cold desert morning wind. I take it in, smuggle it under my coat. With my booty I go back to Roberto's coffee place where Eugenia is still setting up the chairs.

- "Hola! Look what I found!"

I want to show her the lost puppy, feeling heroic as if I had just rescued it from a house on fire. But she does not even turn over. She goes about the room, pulling down chairs, cleaning tables. Eugenia is grumpy today. Grumpy and ugly. I wait for a while, still standing, the puppy stretching at my feet.

- "Where's Roberto?"
- "En casa. He's not feeling well today."

She frantically scrubs the table with her towel, offering me nothing but her unwelcoming back. Finally, she turns over to me, in tears.

- "Juan. I don't think Roberto is going to last much longer."

She called me Juan. It's serious. She falls into my arms and I hold her tight, stroking her hair till she stops sobbing and sniffing. The dog licks her naked feet in her sandals, trying to bring her comfort. A subtle pain invades my body. This cannot be. He's going to be okay. They're going to be okay.

On the eleventh day, I find a nod in my stomach and a cold stream running through my body. The spirits of the ancient Atacamenians have woken up and they whisper in my ears. They take my hand and guide my steps.

"Ven." Come, says the wind at night while the yellow beams of the post lamps tremble and bang their metal chains.

Do I believe in spirits?

I distinctively hear Roberto's voice. "Ven" it says. I can't. I'm nobody. A patient in a waiting room sipping on coffee to pass the time. This is ridiculous; he does not want me there!

"Ven" says the voice, but it sounds different now. Softer. A voice that comes from afar, strangely familiar. I see myself running after a rusty Chevrolet, chasing the voice. "Ven, *hijo*. Ven."

The post lamps fade away but I follow the road, the stars hovering far above. A blanket of stars. They trace lines in the dust. Their invisible feet caress the ground. Their invisible heads salute dark butterflies. I can see them, the butterflies, flapping their paper wings, burning their ephemeral lives away.

I wake up in tears and sweat. I get up, entranced, a force pulling me to the outside. I walk under the million stars shedding light on the path running in between the sand hills and the volcanos. I follow the dark butterflies into the moon-lit desert. I walk, barefoot, feeling the ground beneath my feet, I'm nine again, playing in the dust, chasing bugs and butterflies. The wind carries my father's voice murmuring "ven", urging me to follow it into the heart of the desert. Finally the voice disappears into a thread of air, the butterflies evaporate in the void, leaving me alone under the immensity of the stars, galaxies, constellations imperceptibly swaying over my head. I fall to my knees, suddenly feeling the cold of the night impregnating my bones; I fall down to the ground, an empty carcass. I feel my father's soul flowing away. I grate the soil with my bare hands. I dig into the ground like a damned man. "Where are you dad? Where are you going? Why are you leaving me again?" Heavy drops of tears fall on my nervous hands. Ploc. Ploc. My father's image transforms into that of an older man. Salt-and-pepper hair, veins running through his arms, revealing his thinness.

"Roberto!"

"Robertooooo…"

On the twelfth day, at dawn, I jump into a cab from Calama's train station to the hospital. I yell at the receptionist "I'm a surgeon. I need to see Roberto right now. Roberto Rojas." I don't care that she asks me to wait, I'm already taking the stairs, four by four. I'm a surgeon. I can save him.

Roberto is pale and weak. The nurses are prepping him for surgery. "I'm a surgeon! His surgeon!"

- "Sorry Sir. We have to take him to the O.R. now. He'll be fine. Don't worry."
- "Please let me in. I need to be with him."

From his bed Roberto moans and extends a shivering hand in my direction.

- "Juan. *Calmáte*. I'm glad you came."
- "You called me didn't you? I heard you. In my dreams…"
- "I did indeed. I needed to talk to you before I go."
- "You're not going anywhere Roberto! They'll take care of you, you'll see."
- "Maybe they will, Juan. And maybe they won´t. Either way, I've got something from you."

He nods at a nurse. She nods back and softly opens the bedside table with religious calm and care. She pulls out a set of key, walks around the bed and hovers them in front of me.

-    "Take them, Juan. The place is yours now."

I take the keys, unable to find words. I have no words or thoughts left. I watch the trolley bed roll away, Roberto gently nodding at me, the nurses pushing him along the corridor, through the double doors, through the past, present and future, and into the white light.

"Please, don't go. Don't leave me."

"Papa!"

"Papaaaa!"

There is no ceremony, no mass. Just a straightforward cremation where we stand watching the flames lick the wood of the coffin, taking away Roberto Rojas, his flesh, his voice, his memories. Eugenia cries the loss of the adopted grand-father; I cry the loss of the father I so shortly had; the puppy falls asleep at our feet, enjoying the warmth and the quiet.

I ride back to San Pedro with Eugenia sleeping like a kid, curled up in the back seat, her head on my lap. We met only a few days ago and a generation sets us apart, yet here we are, sharing the same grief and the same uncertain future. I pull the keys from my pocket and wonder: "is this destiny?" I came to the desert looking for a black panther. Instead, I found a lost puppy, a youthful friend and the memory palace of a lovable old man's past. Is this destiny?

I look down at Eugenia's slim body breathing quietly. The puppy is playing with her heavy black hair unravelling like a waterfall down the seat. I feel overwhelmed with how much I came to care about those two lives in so little time. I look at them and I know I want to protect them, watch them smile when they are happy and pout when they are sad. I see the puppy run around the coffee shop, hiding behind the statues and pots, and Eugenia chasing after him, laughing and chirping. I see me, behind the counters, serving the tourists, chatting with the travelers, making *real* coffee for Luisa who may or may not one day come.

When I look back at my life, I realize this should have been the story of either a drunkard or a warrior. Dictatorship, oppression, murder, treason. These should forge only heroes and delinquents. The ones who fight back, and the ones who boil with rage. These should mold exiled soul, tormented by a return, a vengeance, a search for justice. Yet I look back and I don't see either. I know heroes. They work in hospitals every day. Some save the lives they couldn't save back then, when their fathers and uncles were taken away, proudly shouting Allende's name and cursing the rich. Others save the lives they couldn't save, back then, when their fathers and uncles were shooting their brothers in the back, obediently responding to orders. They work together, they never talk about what brought them there. Then they go back to their respective home, far away from each other. One to the East, and one to the West. One up to the mountains where he can absorb their pure innocent majesty, maybe feeling he deserves it, that car, that house, that respect. After all, he saves lives. The other down towards the ocean, but there's no ocean to be seen. He can only look in its direction and wonder: how many corpses are still sleeping in its depth?

If I think about it I could have easily ended up a drunkard, giving the finger to the Guzmans and the Subercaseaux. All those big name which make them feel so important. I was born an Araya, my father didn't build a castle. My father didn't run any big business nor did he own any land. My father was a desperate man who was killed trying to provide for his family. Under the dictatorship he was called a political dissident. Under the democracy he became a terrorist. Different words, same distress.

I should be boiling with rage, drawing the sword and defending my father's honor. But I look down at Eugenia and the puppy and I feel no anger. I let it evaporate and fly away to the mountains' tops; I let it sink at the bottom of every ocean. I think about all the Chiles, all the Palestines, Italies, and Afghanistans. All those countries torn apart by the greed of powerful men high above, executioners of faceless victims, victims of nameless executioners. All those nations dancing at the rhythm of graduated puppeteers. Chicago boys, religious gurus, media-made snake-charmers, avid energy companies. Will we ever rebel? And how? How should our rebellion be? Should we take to the streets and shout our rage, or should we turn our TVs off and block them off, making them irrelevant, puny fools like those truth-sellers standing on soap box in Hyde Park?

Of course I know the answer. After so many years defying the almighties, changing fates, playing God, challenging His power, trying to make Him pay back for the life He'd taken from me, I finally found the perfect vengeance: I got happy. I got happy in the face of the soldiers who ruined my childhood, in the face of the politicians who blinded my teenage years, in the face of the businessmen who abused so many workers who ended up under my scalpel. I got happy in the face of every well-endowed man who expects the poor to be poor and the voiceless to be voiceless.

I got happy despite it all. And so I win.

I open the door to Roberto's café, letting my new found family in.

- "I know how I'm going to call the dog."
- "Oh yeah?" asks Eugenia, her eyes still moist from the sleep and the tears.
- "Happy. His name is happy."
- "Sounds perfect, boss!"

And she smiles at me.

ABOUT THE AUTHOR

Melina Nardi was born in the picturesque town of Namur in the south of Belgium. French through her mother and Italian through her father, Melina is the heir of a long history of immigration. A born traveler, she moved to Italy at the age of seventeen to obtain her B.A. in Performing Arts and her M.A. in Human Rights. She developed an expertise in marketing for NGO and worked in Italy, Germany, USA and Palestine in conflict resolution projects and peace-building initiatives. After spending four years in Washington DC, where she obtained her MBA in Social Entrepreneurship, Melina moved to Chile, following her heart. Since 2011, she's been living and working in Santiago de Chile. She's now an established fiction writer and the proud owner of a small but cozy cultural coffee place for artists and travelers alike.

www.ingramcontent.com/pod-product-compliance
Lightning Source LLC
Chambersburg PA
CBHW060405260626
47160CB00006B/2435